Adriana Trigiani

... Um ... Why am I STILL doodling?

Book rating out of 5 stars ...

3½ stars / 5 stars LOL!

SIMON AND SCHUSTER

First published in Great Britain in 2011 by Simon and Schuster UK Ltd
A CBS COMPANY.
Simon & Schuster UK Ltd
1st Floor, 222 Gray's Inn Road, London WC1X 8HB

www.simonandschuster.com

Originally published in the USA in 2011 by HarperTeen an imprint of HarperCollins Publishers, 10 East 53rd Street, New York, NY 10022.

A CIP catalogue record for this book is available from the British Library.

ISBN 978-0-85707-020-3

1 3 5 7 9 10 8 6 4 2

Printed in the UK by CPI Cox & Wyman, Reading, Berkshire RG1 8EX

For my beloved librarians,

Billie Jean Scott

James Varner

And in memory of

Ernestine Roller

ØNE

THERE IS NO BETTER PLACE ON EARTH THAN RIGHT here on my stoop on 72nd Street in Bay Ridge. Borough of Brooklyn. City of New York. County of Kings. The Empire State.

Home.

I lift my video camera, flip to Record, and peer through the lens, taking in every familiar detail of our cul-de-sac (that's French for *dead end*).

Dad and Mom picked me up at the Prefect Academy in South Bend, Indiana, yesterday morning. After we loaded up the car, I said good-bye to my roommates. Suzanne took pictures of us with her phone. (Casual observation: Beautiful blondes like Suzanne are as comfortable behind the camera taking pictures as they are in front of it.)

Romy, who we are so proud of, because out of the four of us, she has the most athletic ability and made the field hockey team champions, gave me a good-bye gift: a set of Twilight books, and her favorite Lauren Conrad novel: *L.A. Candy.* (Again, an unofficial poll, but jocks at Prefect read a lot. They have to have something to pass the time when they're in the gym on the elliptical.)

Marisol was so sad that she cried, and swore she'd miss me the most. We got to be *very* close friends. Marisol may be the most sensitive girl on the planet, and she is also a true-blue friend. We created our own friendship crest, a puffy heart with a pair of Lady Gaga sequin-studded sunglasses in the center. In a ribbon underneath: *Veritas Forevertas: La chica amica e bono*—or, Forever True: Girlfriends and Goodness.

The four of us had been there for one another the entire school year, so we fell into familiar patterns, like four sisters, even in our good-byes. Suzanne joked around and cheered Marisol up, while Romy reassured her that we would all stay in touch no matter *what.* We made plans to stay in constant communication, by texting, calling, and of course, by Skype and by email. We will remain close in cyberspace.

My roommates made my ninth-grade year at the Prefect Academy as good as it could possibly be, but I'm not going back next year. It's time to be a New Yorker again, attend LaGuardia High School, and reunite with my old friends. I did well on my admissions testing (thank you, Prefect prep class), and Mom and Dad made sure that my application was turned in so that I'd be accepted. My short movie that placed in the Midwest competition sealed the deal; the film faculty thought it was pretty good.

Of course I will miss the big events at Prefect, including the dorm parties, the hayrides, and the film competition, but it's the little things I will treasure when I think of my roommates. I'll never forget the blue streaks in Romy's red hair, which grew out inch by inch until the blue was just a fringe on the bottom like a dust ruffle on a bed. I never had to use an alarm clock because every morning when Marisol weighed herself, the scale blurted out the number and woke me up. I'll miss Suzanne's ability to center part her hair without having to look in the mirror—it was a feat that amazed me until the last day of school.

There was also lot of natural beauty to savor in South Bend, Indiana, once I decided it wouldn't kill me to like another place almost as much as New York City. The Midwest can be mysterious and grand. I'll never forget the slow curves of the Saint Joe River, the twilight sky that turned from electric blue to purple as the sun set, and the snow, so heavy and persistent that it altered the landscape, making mountains of white drifts on the flat cornfields.

Mom, Dad, and I decided to drive through the night, instead of stopping in a motel somewhere in Pennsylvania to break up our trip. We wanted to be together again, just the three of us, in the cocoon of our car on the long highway home. Our family is like a small machine that can't run properly when one of the parts is missing. It turns out that they wanted to get home to Brooklyn as much as I did. A year in Afghanistan made them appreciate everything about our lives in the Chesterton family, including our car and the smooth highways that connect everything. Dad took my mom's hand in the front seat a lot when he was driving. We made it back by two a.m., and I wasn't one bit tired.

This is my first official installment of *The Viola Reels*, which I am calling *The Return Reels*, as this is my triumphant return to the place I love most in the world, New York, in the season I love best, summer, on the harbor that I adore. My river flows with the waters of creative baptism.

By the way, I heard the term *creative baptism* last night for the first time on an all-night radio show my dad was listening to as we drove through Ohio. Mom was asleep, and Dad was listening to Prince (his favorite) and Taylor Swift (mine). We got tired of both, and Dad turned on the old-fashioned radio. That's when he heard a preacher giving a sermon and became entranced with the minister's cadence.

I did too, as the preacher spoke of the healing power of water. I immediately thought of the harbor, and then extended my new belief system to be grateful for all the things I treasure about city life, including: Andrew Bozelli (BFFAA), Caitlin Pullapilly (we have to work around her strict parents, but she's worth it!), Serendipity frozen hot chocolate, the E train, Tag Nachmanoff, 8th Street in Greenwich Village, the Angel tree at the Metropolitan Museum of Art at Christmastime, the Broadway line of the M4 bus, Original Ray's pizza by the slice. I could probably double this list, but that's not the big news.

The headline for today, June 15, 2010: I am finally, completely, and decidedly *home*.

I take a slow pan of our building, drinking in the delicate details that I did not for a single moment forget when I was in boarding school. I shoot the expanse of the lacy wrought-iron fence that separates our stoop from the neighbors, the old blue urn, with cracks that look like spiderwebs in the glaze, and finally the brass mail slot with a Greek key design around the edges. I lift the camera to frame the shot with green, leafy branches that bend gently over our stoop. I widen out to take in the expanse of our street.

Brownstone buildings, just like ours, from the 1800s line either side of my block, shaded by old Norway maple trees that form a summery satin canopy over the old macadam. The sidewalk curbs are staggered with seams of bright yellow paint to define parking spots.

Parking spots cannot be reserved by just anyone. The tenants on our block know that the space in front of their homes officially belongs to them. We actually chase off people who try to park here who do not live on our street. We reserve the spaces as seriously as the guards who protect the money bags on the Brink's truck.

I angle in on the old fire hydrant, once painted in bold stripes of bright red, white, and green in honor of the Italian flag. Now, after years of sun and wear, the hydrant has faded to a dull pink, gray, and mint green. I asked Mom if we could repaint it, and she said, "Let's not. It's symbolic of a bygone era." She's right. These are monuments, after all, Brooklyn monuments. We live in history. Dad says we are caretakers of this old building, and if we keep it in good condition, another family will enjoy it when we have moved on (hopefully never).

The Martinelli family sold our brownstone to my parents eight years ago. They were genuine Italians. We kept the grape arbor and olive trees they planted in the backyard. Our basement smells like a wine bottle, because they used to store crates of grapes there to make wine. In winter, when we build fires, the scent of the Martinellis' homemade wine still wafts through the house, smoky and cold and woodsy, like the wooden barrels they stored it in.

Last night, when we arrived and dropped my suitcases and stuff in the front entry, I ran through the entire house, literally stopping in every single room except the basement apartment, which Mom and Dad rent out.

They sublet the building to a professor and his family on sabbatical while we were gone. The basement apartment is empty, and hopefully that's temporary. My parents are officially worried about money again. Dad and Mom were talking in the car when they thought I was sleeping. I heard Dad say that job number one was renting out the apartment for the summer. We need the income.

Somehow, our money worries don't upset me. Not much anyway. I figure that as long as we're together, our family can figure it out. It's when we're apart, when they're working in faraway places like Afghanistan and

I'm in school in Indiana, *that's* when I get anxious.

Mom thought it was nuts that I had to physically stand in every single room of our house as soon as we got home last night. It was practically dawn, and we were beat, but I didn't care. I had to know that the place was exactly as we left it. I went through the living room, the kitchen, then up the back stairs to my parents' second-floor editing bay and offices, then up to the third floor, where my bedroom and my parents' bedroom share a bath.

There are still lots of things in need of repair: the door with the bashed-in screen that leads to the backyard, the kitchen table with the shaky leg cluttered with stacks of mail, and my bedroom window sash warped by years of rain, which has to be propped open with a ruler. I've asked my dad to fix these things a million times, but now I don't care if he *ever* does. I would take this crumbly old house over any other place in the world. It's a palace to me.

I changed my POV at the Prefect Academy. I'm over complaining about things that don't matter. I'm over asking for stuff I don't really need, or silly things that I want. I don't need anything but home, family, friends, Brooklyn, and my camera. My parents will be *shocked* when they realize how much I've changed.

"Viola!" Andrew waves and shouts from the end of

the block as he turns the corner. I hold up the camera and film him as he comes toward me.

"Andrew?" I holler back. I don't believe my eyes.

Andrew Bozelli, my BFFAA, grew, like I don't know, a *foot* since I've been gone. I've always been really good at judging proportion. I have an almost innate sense of size, placement, and angle when it comes to camera work. But, I'm stunned at the change in Andrew. So totally *stunned,* I actually stop looking through the lens to take in the new version of my old friend. Lean and tall has replaced slight and small in Bozelli world.

Andrew looks *way* older now—practically seventeen, if you had to guess. And, on top of looking older, he turned handsome. His round cheeks went chiseled, his chin lost all its roundness and now appears determined, and since I've been gone, it's obvious he went from shaving once a month to more often.

Besides his height, he has a new look going. His hair has grown out to a very cool length, a straight fringe of coppery reddish brown, long enough to rest over his collar. One familiar trait remains: the freckles all over his nose, which are still there, in the shape of a Band-Aid that's been ripped off.

"Don't film me." Andrew smiles. His braces are off. He left that little detail out of the bazillion texts we do each day. His straight white teeth look new, and just like a television anchor's. His canine teeth, which used to recede, are now in line with the rest of his bite. Dazzling. I switch the camera off and give him a big hug.

"Your braces . . ."

"I know. Gone-zo." He smiles again.

"Olivia Olson gave you a makeover." The mention of Olivia Olson makes him blush; I don't know if that's from love or embarrassment. But one thing is for sure—Andrew snagged the most beautiful girl in the ninth grade as his first girlfriend, so he's set for the rest of high school. They were an official couple for an entire academic year. A huge deal. But I don't want to rehash his entire relationship and eventual breakup with Olivia Olson, so I blurt, "You're all snazzy now."

"Hardly."

"Your hair?"

"Oh yeah, right. The haircut was her idea. And so was the growing out. Olivia said I have a thick neck so I needed longer hair."

"What?" Olivia was way off. I don't even notice a guy's neck. I never once heard Suzanne, Romy, or Marisol ever *mention* a guy's neck.

"My neck is my neck. I figure only girls care about necks. Guys don't at all."

"Right." I'm not going to tell him that I'm a girl and I don't care about necks either. Why pile on?

"Who cares anyway?" Andrew laughs. "You're home."

"I know. I can't even tell you how much I missed Brooklyn."

"You changed too."

"Oh yeah?" I hope it's totally obvious to everyone I meet, including Mrs. Ramos at the bodega, that I had a boyfriend and survived one year away from home.

"I like your hair," Andrew says.

"I had to grow out my bangs. It was almost impossible. They were feisty."

Andrew throws his head back and laughs.

"What's so funny?"

"The way you use words. I don't know. It doesn't come across in emails or texts. I missed it."

"Oh, so now you're Sir Sophisticated."

"Hardly. I'm just saying that I missed your colorful use of the English language."

"Man, someone's been training for the PSATs."

"I know. Mom signed me up for the course. I have this McDullard guy come over once a week."

"Give me his number. I need Mr. McDullard."

"His name is Chang. I call him McDullard."

"So maybe we can take PSAT prep together?"

"Sure." Andrew shrugs.

"I have about a million things I want to do this summer."

"Well, then, we have to cram them in. My parents signed me up for camp."

"Sleepaway?" I know I must sound disappointed.

"Yeah. I don't want to go, but they're making me. I leave in three weeks. It's in Maine. I'll die up there. Eaten to death by mosquitoes. Hospitalized for salmonella from raw hot dogs. Or I'll drown in the lake. It's a freakin' obstacle course of disaster."

Andrew is a total city person and is annoyed instead of awed by the wonders of the great outdoors. Clearly, his parents are trying to make him into something he's not: a camper. Parents who raise their kids in the city believe we should have fresh air in the summer, be surrounded by trees, and paddle canoes. Does it occur to them that we like our city life? I like my trees in pots, not forests. And I like my canoes (for rent) in Central Park. And most of all, I like my hot dogs from a steam bath in a vendor cart, where I know they've been cooked for twelve hours minimum.

"You just ruined my entire summer with that news." I fiddle with the lens on my camera as I try to bring my feelings into focus. For a split second I feel bad that I'm being selfish, but I've been gone nine and a half months, and I thought Andrew and I would spend every moment of the summer doing the stuff we love to do. There's no hassle with Andrew, and yet he's not some pushover, either. And even though we emailed and Skyped when I was in boarding school, it wasn't the same as hanging out. I missed my BFFAA in person, where I can see what he's thinking when he's not saying anything, or we can laugh because of the expressions on our faces, and not in our texts—with a file of smiling faces in various emotional states to punctuate our cyberspace conversations.

"But we'll be in school together in the fall." He grins. "Did you go online and do your schedule?"

"Yep. Thank you for the tips."

"We should find out in early August if we got all our classes together. Caitlin decided to sign up for website advertising and design."

"I can't believe her mom lets her take anything but music theory and advanced violin technique."

"She probably figures Caitlin needs to know how to create her own online ads when she winds up at Carnegie Hall." Andrew stretches out his long legs, so long they practically reach from the second step on the stoop down to the sidewalk. He turns and looks at me. "So, what are your plans?"

"I have to regroup. Now that you're going away, I might have to actually come up with something to fill the days."

"Hey, guys!" Caitlin Pullapilly breaks into a run when she sees Andrew and me on the stoop. Her long black hair sails behind her like a silky veil. She really is the most beautiful girl in Brooklyn or anywhere else. She's a mermaid on dry land.

Caitlin takes the brownstone steps two at a time to hug me. "Boy, did we miss you."

"I missed you, too."

"I love your hair," she says, as she turns my shoulders to check out how long it has grown in the back.

"Viola grew out her feisty bangs." Andrew looks at me and smiles, as though he couldn't wait to repeat that phrase, it delights him so.

"The bangs took, like, nine months. But I'm not the only one." I point to Andrew's hair to get him back. I turn to Caitlin. "So tell me absolutely everything, and don't leave out anything."

"There's so much going on, I don't even know where to start. I got a summer job." Caitlin smooths her capris, embroidered with different diamond shapes in shades of blue.

"A *job*?" I say it like it's the worst news since they canceled *The O.C.*

"I know. My mom is making me," Caitlin says.

Besides being the mother with the *most* rules, and by the way, she makes up new ones on the fly, now it turns out that Mrs. Pullapilly is also a real slave driver. She doesn't let Caitlin do anything—she has to sign up in her own home to use the computer, whose screen faces Mrs. Pullapilly's desk, so zero privacy. And Caitlin can't IM or text until college. The cell phone she gave Caitlin is one of those cheesy for-emergency-only cell phones, which can dial 911 or Mrs. P's personal cell phone only. It's insane.

"Mom wants me to do something all summer so my brain doesn't turn to mush," Caitlin says defensively.

"So what's the job?" I ask.

"I'm going to do all the filing at our dentist's office. He's a good friend of our family. Dr. Balu."

"His partner, Dr. Desloges, did my braces," Andrew says.

I couldn't wait to break out of boarding school to come home and hang with my friends. Now that I'm here, it turns out the Bozellis and the Pullapillys decided that it was best to keep Andrew and Caitlin so busy, they'd hardly have time for me. I forget that parents in general still make decisions for their teenage kids. My parents made me go to boarding school, and even though I didn't have a choice in the matter, once I got there, I was on my own. I had an entire school year of making every decision for myself, so it's pretty weird to come home and find that my friends hardly make any for themselves.

I had big summer plans for the three of us. Meals included. I wanted to order in sesame noodles and eat them on the roof. We'd take the water taxi to the South Street Seaport, sail a couple of 360s around Manhattan on the Circle Line, and take bike rides in Prospect Park. Dad said he'd drive us to Far Rockaway beach during the week to avoid crowds, and to Coney Island on Saturdays. I was even going to ask my mom to drive us to Jersey to Great Adventure. But now all my plans just blew up like a bald tire on a hot road. Here's the summer: Andrew decides to temporarily relocate to Maine while Caitlin disappears as an indentured servant at a dental office. And I'm alone.

"I've still got a few weeks before camp starts," Andrew reasons.

"I don't start working until a week from Monday," Caitlin explains.

"We'll just have to cram a lot in," I tell them. My mind begins to race with possibilities. I'll have to put my plans on turbo, and fill the days before Andrew and Caitlin disappear into camp and work.

"Whatever you want to do." Caitlin shrugs.

"I want to have dinner tonight on the roof. Cold sesame noodles and Stewart's root beer and mini mint chip cheesecakes from Junior's."

"Sorry to interrupt you guys," Mom says, holding the front door open with her foot. "Well, look at this. The old stoop is back to normal." My mom beams. "And I'm loving it."

Even after that long car ride, my mom looks beautiful, or maybe I just missed her so much that she seems lovelier than ever. She has her hair piled on her head with bobby pins. Her rhinestone-studded reading glasses dangle around her neck like crown jewels. Her brown hair is almost red now, fried from the Afghan sun. She is still no fashionista. Her boyfriend jeans are hiked up with a canvas belt that's lost its grommets from wear. That's my mom. No frills *and* she gets the last bit of use out of whatever she has, whether it's a tube of toothpaste, a jar of peanut butter, or a canvas belt. "The long-awaited reunion."

"Yep," Andrew says, flipping his bangs to the side and off his face.

"I like that haircut, Andrew," Mom says.

"Thanks, Mrs. Chesterton."

"I thought we'd cook out tonight in the backyard," Mom says.

"Oh man, we were going to order in," I complain.

"You can order in anytime. This is a special night. Dad is firing up the old grill. You know what that means. . . ."

"Red hamburgers and black hot dogs?" I joke.

"Your father is very proud of his grilling. And I try not to complain when he does the cooking. We don't want to discourage your father doing chores—*ever*. Got it?" Mom says. She looks at Andrew and Caitlin. "And of course, you two are welcome to stay."

"Thanks," Caitlin and Andrew say politely. How can they resist a lame cookout?

"Grand is coming over, and she's bringing George," Mom says.

"Oh, hallelujah. I love that guy. Wait till you meet him, Caitlin. He looks like Cary Grant."

Caitlin actually knows who Cary Grant is, not because she's a film buff but because black-and-white movies are some of the only ones that her mother lets her watch. Mrs. P liked *The Philadelphia Story* and *The Awful Truth*. Turns out they actually enjoy Golden Age of Hollywood slapstick in India. Mrs. Pullapilly doesn't know about the racy black-and-white movies made pre–Hayes Code in 1930s Hollywood, but if she did, I'm sure she'd ban them from Caitlin's eyeballs.

"Is George really as handsome as Cary Grant?" Caitlin asks.

"Swear." I turn to Andrew. "You remember George—he was in my movie project at Prefect."

"Good actor," Andrew says.

I look up at my mom, who watches the three of us with a look of total joy on her face. I may have missed her, but she sure missed me—and my friends. "Do you think Grand is going to marry him?"

"I hope not. I'm too old to be in another wedding party. But you never know. Love is funny that way. It just sneaks up on you."

"And then it ruins your life," Andrew says.

Mom throws her head back and laughs. "Don't be bitter, Andrew."

"Too late. I have the haircut to prove it," Andrew says.

This is one of the things I like best about Andrew. He has already healed from his breakup with Olivia Olson, even though he is the one who initiated the proceedings. He'll never be one of those people who lets emotions pile up and then has to sort through them (like me). Andrew doesn't hold grudges, nor does he look back and wish things were different. It's good to have a sensible BFFAA.

"I could use a couple of potato peelers in the kitchen," Mom says as she goes.

"Let's give your mom a hand," Caitlin says, always eager to please authority figures.

I follow Andrew and Caitlin into the house. I can't believe it, my first day back—and the summer I have imagined and so carefully planned, detail by detail, is *not happening!* All my dreams of endless summer afternoons on the roof, hanging out and talking and making movies with my friends, have just gone up in a puff of black smoke, as dark and opaque as the ones off my dad's grill.

Oh well. Time to regroup. I learned that working with actors on my movie. When you don't get exactly what you want as the director, roll with it, because if you don't, the joy goes right out of the process. *Stay loose and cool* will be my mantra this summer. I can do that. Happily. As long as I'm in Brooklyn, do I really have *any* problems?

I may retire my Princess Snark tiara for good. The truth is, I've outgrown it. Marisol taught me that the glass half full can really quench your thirst if you let it. And when I analyze the situation and look around at my life, I got what I wanted most: I'm home.

TWO

CAITLIN HELPS ME DRAPE THE PRESSED RED-AND-white-checked tablecloth over the picnic table. Andrew, who is helping Dad, is trying not to hack too much as Dad sends smoke through the borough while fanning the grill.

"There we go," Dad announces. "The briquettes have caught fire."

"Adam, remember the ozone layer," Mom says cheerfully to Dad through the hole in the screen door.

"I'm more worried about my lungs," Andrew jokes, trying to find a pocket of clean air to breathe by the olive tree.

"Stay back then, buddy boy," my father tells him. "Downwind is a killer."

"Hell-loo!" Grand says as she comes down the walkway from our street to the backyard. Her sunhat is so wide, I can barely see George behind her. She waits for him to reach around her to open the gate.

Grand sashays into the backyard like it's a theatrical set and she's making her entrance playing Queen Victoria. She fluffs her full cotton ruffled skirt behind her like a train. *"La famiglia!"* She extends her arms.

I rush over to Grand and throw my arms around her. Mom comes out of the kitchen carrying the biggest bowl of potato salad I've ever seen.

"Your signature potato salad. Yum!" Grand says.

"Thanks, Ma." Mom kisses Grand on the cheek. "I fussed." And it's true. Mom decorated the potato salad with a sunburst made with slices of hard-boiled egg and rays of red paprika.

Dad waves at them with his tongs through his fog of smoke.

Grand gives me a box of cupcakes.

"They're from Sweetiepie in the Village. Far better bakers than I."

George greets my mom as a little dog (!), a King Charles spaniel, nips at his heels.

Grand leans down and picks up the dog. "Say hello to your first cousin Cleo."

"You got a *dog*?" I can't believe it. Grand is so *not* an animal person, and not because she doesn't like dogs. We come from a family who never has pets because we're always traveling: Gram with her plays and Mom and Dad with their work. Sure, we get wistful when we see kittens in a rescue crate on the street corner, or new puppies on a leash, but we know our limits. The artist's life is no place for pets.

"Mom, you're forever full of surprises." Mom reaches down to pet Cleo.

"Cleo is a gift from my George," Grand says, practically exploding with love.

"I adore puppies," Caitlin sighs. She pets Cleo but looks at George instead. It's like it's 1940 and she's meeting the real Cary Grant.

"She's a sweetie," George says.

"Well, here's how it went. The story of Cleo." Grand removes her sunhat and hangs it on the hook on the grape arbor. "We were on the road. Youngstown, Ohio?"

"Cincinnati," George corrects her gently.

"Right. Right. George said, 'We need a dog.' And I said, 'George, a dog is not a *need*, a dog is a *want*.' And he said, 'Wouldn't it be great to have a little companion on the road?' So, we went to the shelter there, because I saw that puppy mill episode on *Oprah* and it broke my heart. I will never, as long as I live, get those images out of my mind. I felt compelled to *do* something. Anyhow. There we are at the pound, and you should have seen the dogs. I wanted to adopt them *all*. But the lady running the place said, 'I have the perfect dog for you, the owner died, that's tragic, but she's only three and very well behaved.' Then she brought us to Cleo. And I fell in love and then George fell in love, and here she is."

Cleo's brown eyes are so big and wet, she seems emotionally moved by Grand's story, even though we know Grand has probably told this story a million times. Cleo had better get used to it. Actresses tell the same stories over and over again. (Occupational hazard from memorizing lines and repeating them, performance after performance, night after night, in city after city.)

"She's already brought us luck." George smiles. His perfect teeth are so white, they are almost blue Hollywood dazzlers. "The best kind of luck."

"How so?" Dad brings a platter of his signature summer cookout black hot dogs and red hamburgers to the table. Mom hands George and Grand beer from the ice chest.

"Oh, George, let me tell," Grand implores him.

"The floor is yours, Corrie."

Mom shoots me a look. George calls Grand *Corrie*

instead of *Coral*. The last guy who did that, Grand *married*. Mom better not retire her teal matron/daughter-of-honor gown just yet. And I'd better start scouring the sales racks at Forever 21 for a discount prom dress that will serve as a granddaughter/junior bridesmaid dress. George and Grand's love is as gorpy as my mom's home-made chocolate nut sauce she's going to pour on the sundaes after dinner.

"Let's propose a toast." Grand holds up the bottle.

"Mom, are you getting married again?" My mother cuts to the chase. (She told me that's her new philosophy since she turned forty-five: Just ask.)

George and Grand laugh.

"No, no. I've found my soul mate. I don't need a husband."

Mom exhales and swigs her beer. Crisis averted!

"It's news of work." Grand looks up at George. "Together. *Arsenic and Old Lace* is going to Broadway!" Grand actually gets tears in her eyes as she makes the announcement.

"And we're keeping our roles. New director—but he loved what he saw in Cleveland, and here we go," George says.

"Wow, they're bringing an old chestnut back to life," Dad says.

"Sometimes old chestnuts are the sweetest," Grand snaps.

She ought to know. Grand has been in every old play from *Machinal* to *Bell, Book, and Candle*. She could make a necklace out of old chestnuts.

"Congratulations, Mom." Mom gives Grand a big hug. My mother has spent a lot of her life worried about Grand and her crazy life in the American theater. The life of the actress can be horrible: long stretches of no work, and then long stretches of a lot of work for very little pay. But Grand loves acting, and Mom would rather see her be busy and happy than unemployed and bored, so she has learned to keep her fingers crossed during the in-between times when Grand can't land a job.

"Daryl Roth—she's a great producer—flew out, dressed head to toe in Chanel bouclé, shoes too . . . ," Grand says.

"Petite. Blond. Beautiful," George agrees.

"You would have noticed that, George," Grand teases. "Anyhow, Daryl saw the show and said, 'This is exactly what the doctor ordered. *This* is what people want to see: a glorious American classic with humor.' That's what she told us anyhow." Grand sits. Cleo jumps up onto the picnic bench next to her. "I mean, how lucky can we be? The right play, the right producer, in the exact right moment."

"This is a once-in-a-lifetime confluence of luck," Dad says.

"You got that right, Adam," Grand agrees.

"They're bringing in a director from England, Les Longfellow," George says. "Les needs a summer rental. Let us know if you hear of anything."

"Our downstairs apartment is available," Mom says.

"What happened to the professor who was living here?" Grand asks.

"His sabbatical is up. He went back to Wisconsin," Dad says.

"Les is in a hotel in midtown, but he doesn't like it." George looks at Grand.

"He'd love it here. Just give him our number." Mom looks at Dad.

"Can do." Grand feeds a bit of black hot dog to Cleo. "Now." Grand turns to Andrew, Caitlin, and me. "Tell me your summer plans."

"I'm working at the dentist's office," Caitlin offers.

"Teeth are important," Grand says.

"Like windows on a house. You can't have a beautiful building with cracked windowpanes and rotting sashes. The same goes for teeth."

"I had my teeth sealed when I was eight," Andrew says.

"And what are your summer plans?"

"I'm going to camp in Maine. I don't like nature, but I think the fresh air might do me some good." Andrew has black soot around his nostrils from Dad's grill.

Grand turns to me. "How about you?"

"I got nothin'." And it hits me. I really do have nothing. Now my summer seems like a long stretch of unplanned days that my mother will fill up with chores like cleaning out closets, or logging footage on the Avid, or my dad with stuff like painting walls and planting the yard.

"You *must* have a summer project."

Mom sits down next to me on the picnic bench. "Your grand is a great believer in the summer project. I learned knitting one summer, decoupage another. And then there was modern dance in the city and fly-fishing camp in the great north woods of Wisconsin."

"I was doing summer stock in Racine. It was convenient," Grand says. "And look, it all paid off. How many film editors can say they know how to bait a hook?"

"I'm nothing if not well rounded." Mom laughs.

"Exactly right. Summer is the time to master a new skill. Endless days roll out in front of you like a highway; you have to fill that road with scenery."

"What could I possibly master?" I think aloud.

"It will come to you," Grand reassures me. "Just think about what you want to say, and the form will follow the function."

"Viola is already the best filmmaker around," Andrew says, always in my corner.

"Thanks, Andrew. I'll stay gone another nine months, and you can call me Lina Wertmüller."

I take a bite of one of my dad's signature hot dogs, charred to black on the outside and yet still cold on the inside. Dad looks at me for my approval, and I say, "Delish" through the bite, even though this dog is far from tasty. Who cares about the cuisine anyhow? I wouldn't care if Dad BBQ'd shoes on the grill and served them medium rare. I'm just happy to be home, surrounded by my good friends and nutty family—and then of course, George Dvorsky, who looks like he just might be around for the long haul.

Mom carries the old Lasko fan into my bedroom. I'm texting Andrew, making plans for Mermaid Day, our favorite event at Coney Island. "I don't need the fan, Mom. But thanks."

"It's awfully hot in here."

"I can stand it. I survived boarding school, remember?"

Mom sits down next to me. She smooths the turquoise

and white comforter over the edge of the bed. "I'm so happy we're all home again."

"Did it seem like years to you?"

"Decades. But you'll understand that when you're a mother. You want your baby near you always. No matter how old she grows. It's just the way it is."

"You know what's weird?"

"That your dad thinks he's a great cook?"

We laugh.

"It's weird that I miss my roommates. I miss Marisol. Suzanne too. And even Romy—though she's a jock and was always at practice. I didn't think I'd miss them so much. Every night, we'd walk back from the dining hall together and talk through our days. No matter what, we all connected at the end of the day and talked about all the stuff that was going on and what papers were due and how our classes were going. It was like having sisters."

"I know you've missed out on that." Mom gets the worry crease between her eyes.

"But that's what's so funny. Once I got to boarding school, I had instant sisters. I was so anxious to leave Indiana I didn't think about who I'd leave behind."

"Email them," Mom suggests. "That's why all those brilliant programmers invented all those gizmos. So people like you could have instant pen pals. When I was a girl, we mailed letters to France. It took weeks to get a reply."

Mom angles the fan in my window and turns it on low. Then, as she turns to go, she puts her arms around me and gives me a hug.

Dad stands in the doorway. "Good night, Vi."

Mom gets up and gives Dad the corner of the bed. He sits.

"Good night, Dad."

"Those burgers were pretty awesome, don't you think?"

It never ceases to amaze me how insecure my father is when it comes to grilling. "The best," I reassure him. Mom stands in the doorway and rolls her eyes.

"I love my girl," he says, and gives me a hug and a kiss.

"I love you, Dad."

As Mom and Dad go to their room, I hear them whisper.

I IM Marisol.

Me: Home twelve hours, had a cookout—Andrew and Caitlin over, Grand got a dog.

MC: You weren't kidding, more stuff happens in Brooklyn than anywhere else!

Me: No kidding.

***MC:** I unpacked and went to Friendly's with my family. It always smells like spilled milk at our Friendly's, but the sundaes are delish.*

Me: I miss you guys.

***MC:** I know! I can't believe it. How is Andrew?*

Me: He got cute.

***MC:** How cute?*

Me: Tall. Braces off.

***MC:** Everybody here in Richmond is the same size they were a year ago.*

Me: Sorry.

***MC:** Did Andrew say anything about Olivia?*

Me: It's still over. There are no lasting effects except the haircut. He's the same old Andrew. Sigh of relief.

***MC:** Suzanne e'd that her dad is okay. Not great. Okay.*

Me: Is she worried?

***MC:** She was low-key, but I can tell she's worried. We had some laughs because Romy is still in love with Kevin. Romy has been emailing Suzanne nonstop, hoping for a news flash on Kevin. Suzanne told Romy that Kevin still has a girlfriend. But Romy doesn't care. She's determined. FYI: Kevin's girlfriend is from Ireland.*

Me: Exotic.

***MC:** I think I have a job at Target this summer.*

Me: Everybody's getting jobs!

MC: Need the money.

Me: Who doesn't?

MC: LOL.

I lie back in my bed and listen to the dull whirl of the fan. I lean over and pull the chain on my lamp, shaped like a sheep, which I left at home and didn't take to Prefect because it seemed babyish last year. Funny, now it doesn't seem babyish, it seems kitschy. I think my roommates would have liked it.

I turn over in my bed. It's strange to be alone in my room after a year in the quad. I never thought I would like sharing a room, but there was something nice about coming in after class and debriefing my day with my friends. I actually miss Marisol whispering every detail about our teachers, the classes, and the people in them. Sometimes I'd fall asleep before she finished, but she didn't mind. Suzanne liked to study into the night, while Romy, who always had to get up early for field hockey practice, would go to sleep wearing a satin mask with eyes embroidered on it. If only we all lived in the same city. And if only, in the land of my sweetest dreams, that city could be New York.

* * *

I follow Dad and Mr. Longfellow into our basement apartment. He doesn't seem like a famous director, but more like every dad I know.

Our furnished apartment for rent is downright spectacular.

Mom and I cleaned the apartment, changed the linens, checked the silverware and dishes, and made sure all the appliances were working. We even changed out some of the furniture, bringing down a leather recliner easy chair and a pretty floor lamp. Mom thought it would be a selling point, to have a good reading chair for a theater director. Mom also bought some flowering potted plants, red geraniums and white nettle, placing them around to cheer the place up. English people are known for their gardens, so we went for it! It's officially a cozy one-bedroom garden apartment with a kitchenette, perfect for someone who needs a short-term stay in the city.

"Lovely," Mr. Longfellow says in his British accent.

"There's a garden." Dad shows Mr. Longfellow the way to the slate portico off the back bedroom. Dad hosed down the slate floor and moved small trees in terra-cotta urns to create a wall of privacy between the porch and our backyard. From this vantage point, all you see is green through the French doors from the bedroom. Nice. Mom moved the best of our garden furniture, a wrought-iron table and two deck chairs with white canvas cushions, to the portico. It almost looks like the terrace of a fancy hotel.

"Ah, a garden." Mr. Longfellow's shoulders relax.

"Our last tenant even read the paper out here in the winter."

"It's peaceful," Mr. Longfellow says. "I'm going to need a respite during rehearsals."

Mr. Longfellow is like any of Grand's theater friends. He uses language as it sounds in books, not as it sounds in conversation. He is dramatic in a gentlemanly way, his eyebrows shoot up and down, and he has very deliberate facial expressions. He has a booming voice and fills a room when he enters it. It's sort of a star-quality thing. When I used to ride the subway with Grand, we played a game called Star Quality. We would choose people on the train who we felt had cinematic potential. Here's the list of things you must have to be a star, the SQ specifics:

- Large-size head
- Wet eyes (limpid for camera work; nearsighted people often have the best eyes for film work)
- Wide-set eyes. Eyes too close together are hard to film.

- Great beauty for a woman (full lips, small nose) or
- Obvious masculinity (square jaw, high forehead, hair!) with rough edges for a man
- Deliberate character features (unique nose, expressive mouth)
- When this person enters a room, subway car, or any enclosed place, if everyone looks up at the person simultaneously, that's a sign of star quality. SQ is a mesmerizing presence that draws attention to itself just by existing. SQ is as obvious as it is rare. SQ cannot be manufactured; it has to exist in and wholly of itself.

Les Longfellow looks like one of the guys in the painting of the Last Supper. He has a red beard and short hair. He's taller than my dad but about the same age. "Do you have a roll-away bed for the bedroom?" he wants to know.

"We do."

"I'll need one."

"You can have as much company as you like," my dad says. "Let me show you the basement where we do the laundry."

Mr. Longfellow follows Dad down to the basement.

Mom peeks out the back door. "How's it going?" she asks me.

"He likes it. We have to get the roll-away out of the attic."

"No problem."

Dad and Mr. Longfellow come up from the basement. They discuss good restaurants in Brooklyn. Mr. Longfellow likes Indian food. I'll have to ask Caitlin for up-to-date recommendations. He also likes the occasional Italian farm-table fare (whatever that is).

Dad extends his hand. "It's all yours, Les. Welcome to Brooklyn."

"Thank you." He turns to me. "How old are you, Viola?"

"I'm fifteen."

"That's exactly how old my son is. He's going to spend the summer with me."

"Viola can show him all the sights." Dad smiles and looks at me.

"Sure," I say. The last thing I want is to get stuck with some snobby British boy for the summer, but I'll agree to anything so my parents get a good renter in here. Besides, he might be cute, and I can practice talking to a boy from a foreign country who will not be able to either glom on or dis me at school, depending on his reaction.

Either way, I'm going to be nice to the Longfellows. This is my way of contributing to the family coffers without having to get an actual job. "I'll even introduce him to my friends. We'll find stuff to do."

"Wonderful," Mr. Longfellow says.

Dad gives Mr. Longfellow the keys to the apartment. "I'll move in tomorrow," he says.

I IM Suzanne in Chicago.

Me: **Don't tell me you have a summer job too.**

SS: I do. Dairy Queen.

Me: **Ugh.**

SS: I'll be sick of Blizzards by the end of the summer, but right now, I'm having one a day for free.

Me: **Enjoy.**

SS: Ha.

Me: **Mom and Dad rented the basement apartment to a theater director. He has a son. He is exactly fifteen like us.**

SS: Psychic flash: potential new boyfriend for you.

Me: **I doubt it.**

SS: Your heart belongs to Andrew. I knew it!

Me: **You and Marisol should form a chat room to discuss Andrew and me. No, thankfully, he is over Olivia, which gives us time for our BEST FRIENDSHIP. I would never trade best friend for boyfriend. Ever.**

***SS:** OK. OK. I hear you. What's the British guy's name?*

Me: Maurice. But it's pronounced Morris. When I met Mr. Longfellow, he called me VEE-OH-LA. I didn't correct him because I don't know how much of it is accent related. How's your dad?

***SS:** Some days better than others. He sends his love to you.*

Me: Love right back!

***SS:** I wish you were here.*

Me: I wish YOU were HERE.

I imagine Suzanne at the Dairy Queen. I remember how we loved going to the DQ in South Bend. Peppy Trish loved a dip cone, and she turned all the girls from the East on to them. You have to go way south like Virginia or way north like Vermont for a DQ. I hear there's one in Queens, but that has not been verified.

I wish there was a way to have my roommates from Prefect close, and still live here and keep my friends that I grew up with, all in conjunction, and simultaneously. I imagine there's a world where that could happen, I just have to figure out *how*.

THREE

MRS. PULLAPILLY MAKES A KILLER TANDOORI CHICKEN. Slow cooked, rubbed with spices, and hot, hot, hot, it's a perfect summer meal. Andrew and I will do anything to score a dinner invitation when Mrs. P fires up the clay pots. She also makes this very soft bread, which she throws on the grill, to serve with it. Vegetables are always delish at their house, as they are finely chopped and there's a fresh dressing on them. No matter how many times I ask my mom to try to copy the dressing, it never comes out the way the Pullapillys make it.

The dessert is always amazing. And at the end of the meal, Mr. Pullapilly roasts pineapple and serves it with some kind of vanilla yogurt. "To cool the taste buds," he says.

The Pullapillys live on the outskirts of Bay Ridge in a new Indian section, complete with stores that sell their spices and favorite foods. Their apartment is on the bottom floor of a new apartment building. They have a common garden with the other tenants, which is planted with all sorts of exotic flowers and greens (probably to remind them of the climate they come from). The apartment is decorated in deep green and white, with fabric tapestries on the walls. The living room furniture is low and comfortable. There's a small gurgling tabletop fountain on a side table in the entry.

"You know, Mrs. P, when I was marooned in boarding school, one of my dreams of home involved your tandoori chicken."

Mrs. P laughs. "Well, you and Andrew are my biggest fans. I assure you that my sisters and mother make a far better chicken than I do."

"Let's hope I never taste theirs, because as far as I'm concerned, yours is the best."

"Dad made mint tea," Caitlin says as she pours me a glass and then Andrew.

"Did you miss my mint tea, too?" Mr. P wants to know.

"I sure did."

"Did you get a job for the summer?" Mrs. P asks.

"I'm working on it." It seems no adult on the planet will rest until I get a summer job.

"Dr. Balu went to a lot of trouble to give Caitlin a job."

"I'm very grateful, Mama." She smiles.

"How about you, Andrew?" Mr. P asks.

"I'm going to camp," he says, taking a sip of his tea.

"Wonderful!" Mrs. P says as she serves us the delicious chicken from the clay pot. A mist of spices rises up from the pot, and my mouth waters.

"I don't really want to go."

"The fresh air will be good for you," Mrs. P says.

"That's what I hear," Andrew says agreeably.

I take a taste of the chicken. It's very lean, spicy hot, and so tender I can cut it with my fork. The bite is so delicious, I close my eyes to savor it.

"I'm so happy to be home," I say dreamily. "I missed the international cuisine of Brooklyn."

The Pullapillys laugh. "You're so dramatic, Viola," Caitlin says.

"There are some things in life that are over the top, and this chicken is number one on the list!" I assure them. "The Basmati Palace in South Bend can't compare, trust me."

"So your grandmother is in *Arsenic and Old Lace*? I enjoy revivals. I really liked *Arms and the Man* at the . . ." Mr. P looks at his wife.

"The Classic Stage Company," Mrs. P says.

"My wife is not only my partner, she's my memory."

"We go to so many plays, it's hard to keep up," Mrs. P explains.

"And a lot of musical concerts," Caitlin says.

"That's how you fell in love with music," Mr. P says.

"It helped," Caitlin admits.

"Devica is a lovely flautist," Mr. P says proudly, gesturing to Caitlin's younger sister.

"Do you play an instrument?" I ask Abel, who is ten.

"I play the piano," he says.

"You guys should have your own orchestra," Andrew says.

"Someday," Mr. Pullapilly says. He spoons some cool chopped salad onto my plate; there are cucumbers and tomatoes with a yogurt dressing.

"It's so nice to have you both home," Mrs. Pullapilly says.

Mr. Pullapilly isn't kidding about a band. This is a family of overachievers. They don't just learn an instrument for fun, they aim for Carnegie Hall. Caitlin doesn't read one book by an author, but all of them. The science projects that come out of this house are something to see. Caitlin didn't show up with a barometer made out of a milk carton (like me); she made a cotton gin, engine and all. The Pullapillys play hardball, and they play to win.

The rehearsals for *Arsenic and Old Lace* are "chugging along," Grand says, which is a totally old-fashioned way to describe it, as the play takes place in 1941, the era of the Super Chief and high-speed trans-American trains.

My summer plans have yet to take shape, but I'm working on it. I'm putting together a virtual tour of Grand's career, a kind of mini-documentary, gathering photographs and bits of film she appeared in and weaving them into a story, which I plan to give her on opening night.

Right now I'm working on Grand's résumé picture from 1965. I listen to my voice-over:

"Once actors get over the excitement of getting the part, they wrestle with how to play it. The director's job is to stage the show, but also to bring out the best in each actor. Coral Cerise has worked with some of the greats: Michael Langham, Garland Wright, and now, Les Longfellow."

I click off the audio and begin adjusting Grand's image on the screen. I start in tight close-up and pull back until her full face is revealed. In this shot, she looks a lot like Cleopatra might've looked, big black eyeliner and straight black hair. She definitely has star quality.

There's always a story behind any show Grand appears in. There's always a cliffhanger to the whole thing, and this one is no different—like will or won't Grand win the part, will or won't she win the spot on the coveted bus-and-truck tour, and will or won't the show itself run longer than five performances? Even *Arsenic and Old Lace* wasn't a done deal until the moment the contracts were signed. Grand and George had already worked with one director, who cast them, and they liked her. She was replaced with Les Longfellow when the play went to Broadway. Usually, the director would recast, but Grand and George were very lucky. Mr. Longfellow liked them enough to keep them.

Big whew.

George plays the leading man, Mortimer Brewster, a drama critic. His family is nuts, including two spinster aunts who live in a house in Brooklyn and have taken to poisoning old men with wine that is laced with arsenic. Grand is playing Martha Brewster, one of the old aunts. George has a young love interest in the play, and Grand is not one bit jealous of her. Mom says that's one of the things about Grand that makes her alluring. Grand has self-confidence.

Dad and Mom are totally sucking up to Mr. Longfellow. Anything he needs, he gets. Dad even loaned Mr. Longfellow our Bose CD player. The great director is playing CDs of Victrola-style music constantly, which makes me depressed. It sounds like somebody is hand cranking old records from a Norma Shearer movie, scratches and wah-wahs and all. Evidently, Mr. L isn't listening for pleasure; he is choosing transition music for the play. He is very picky (Grand says), so he's listening to every tune of that era he can get his hands on (George says).

Grand, like all actresses, is that mix of eternally grateful at having a job on Broadway, which makes her humble, and confident that she will do a good job, which makes her seem a little stuck-up. It takes humility *and* guts to be an artist, as she and my parents are quick to remind me. You have to believe in yourself just enough, not too much, and then push until you get what you want.

Mom is already planning what she is going to wear to opening night, which is only six weeks away. Grand always throws a big opening-night party in her apartment after the official party thrown by the producers. She makes casseroles from her Arlene Francis cookbook (Arlene Francis was famous in the 1950s, and Grand was in a play with her once) and sangria from an old recipe she's had for years. People sing, laugh, and smoke at her parties, and leave never having had a better time. Sometimes I think Grand loves her opening-night party more than being in the play.

"Viola, come down. Our guest has arrived," Mom hollers from the bottom of the stairs. I turn off my laptop and slip into Mom's welcome home gift to me: laceless red Converse sneakers. I look in the mirror on my way out, smoothing down my hair, which has gotten awful pouffy in the summer humidity.

"Viola, I'd like you to meet Maurice," Mom says.

I size him up politely without staring or acting too interested, a technique that Suzanne taught me. Basically, you just look away a lot, as if you're aware of everything going on around the boy instead of the boy himself. Using Suzanne's focus and glance technique, it appears that Maurice is a little taller than me, with blond hair that's cut super short. He has green eyes and a good face—definitely not as handsome as Tag Nachmanoff (king of LaGuardia High School and the best-looking boy in the coastal U.S.) but pretty cute for a boy from another country.

"Doesn't Maurice look like Jude Law?" Mom says.

I glare at my mother while Maurice's face turns the color of my sneakers. I can't believe my mother is bringing up way older actors. If anything, Maurice looks a lot like Sterling Knight, but Mom wouldn't know him.

"Welcome to Brooklyn," I tell him.

"It's a pleasure to meet you," he says politely, which is not a shock, because, let's face it, the British are known for their excellent manners.

"I'm going to take Maurice down to the apartment. He came here straight from the airport, and he's very tired."

"Okay."

I race back up to my room two steps at a time and call Caitlin. "He's here," I tell her.

"What's he like?"

"Proper and British. And my mother, I almost died, said he looked like Jude Law."

"Does he?" Caitlin wants to know.

"It wasn't the first thing I thought when I looked at him. I mean, he *sounds* like Jude Law, but so does every British guy."

"I wish he looked like Robert Pattinson," Caitlin says dreamily.

"You are so obsessed with movie stars."

"I know. They seem so perfect to me," Caitlin admits. "I saw *Twilight* seven times," she says proudly.

"Maybe you like movie stars because your mom won't

let you go out with real-life boys."

"Probably. I can't believe you have an actual stranger living in your house. A *guy*. My parents would *never* allow it."

"He's down in the rental, like, two floors away from my room. It's no different from having neighbors in an apartment building. And your mom allows *that*."

"I guess. But you know my mother. It's all in the interpretation."

"Well, suck up to her and get her permission to come over for dinner on the roof."

"Are we ordering in?"

"Yep. Andrew is coming."

"I'll ask."

I get a tired feeling whenever Caitlin has to ask her mom for permission to do anything, because I'm absolutely sure it's going to be a Big No, and that's depressing. Then I hear the bell on my laptop. I'm relieved when Andrew's name pops up.

AB: What's happening?

Me: Incoming.

AB: Your boarder?

Me: Yep. He's here.

AB: I can't come over tonight.

Now I'm totally annoyed. What happened to my friend who couldn't wait for me to get back from boarding school? Was it something I said? Did I grow out my bangs and therefore lose a friend? I'm going to go right out on a limb and ask him why.

Me: Are you serious?

AB: Have to go to Long Island. My cousin's house.

Me: You're leaving me here with a stranger?

AB: Can Caitlin come over?

Me: Not until her mom checks with Homeland Security.

AB: You'll be okay.

Me: Clear the weekend?

AB: Can do.

One thing is for sure about Andrew—if he says he's going to show up, he shows up. But what's bothering me is that he never needed an invitation before, and now it seems like he does. I hope he hasn't become that kind of boy, and therefore I have to be a different kind of girl. I don't want to set myself up for disappointment.

Me: We have things to do before you go to camp. Mermaid Day.

AB: Would not miss it.

Me: Have fun on Long Island.

I had this crazy dream when I was in boarding school. New York City was frozen over in my absence under a clear glass shell, like a snow globe. The skyline was just a bunch of tall, empty buildings with no light coming out of the windows.

Drifts of snow covered the streets; all was silent: no cars and no people. The rivers were solid sheets of silver ice, and you could walk across them. It was only when I became frustrated and hacked a hole in the dome of the snow globe with the needle I had snapped from atop the Empire State Building that the city came back to life.

The sun came out, the snow melted, and people began to appear in the streets. Life as I remembered it resumed in full. I had finally made it back home. The world as I knew it was the same. I woke up relieved.

In real life, the city did not freeze, no one waited for my return, and in general, things went on just fine in Brooklyn without me. Our house was the same. Sal's Pizzeria had the same specials nine months later: one calzone with your choice of two fillings and a soda, five bucks. My friends had a good year. They missed me, and I missed them, but that didn't stop anything; life went on just like normal.

So much for frozen dreams.

"I can come over! And you won't believe it! Mom and Dad gave me permission to spend the night!" Caitlin shouts into the phone. Then she whispers, "I think Mom realizes how much I missed you, and she's being lenient."

"Great," I tell her. "Andrew can't make it."

"Just us?" she says.

"I'm going to invite Maurice up for dinner. Mom is, like, totally making me responsible for him."

"No problem," Caitlin says.

"There won't be if you don't say anything to your parents. Do *not* tell your mother there will be a foreign guy here. If you do, she'll have him frisked and bodyguards sent over, or even worse, she'll keep you at home."

"Got it."

Here's what I love about cold sesame noodles from Sung Chu Mei. First of all, they feature two of my favorite foods: pasta and peanuts. Dad says there aren't actual peanuts in the sauce—that it's sesame I'm tasting—but to me, cold sesame noodles taste like creamy, but spicy, peanut butter on spaghetti. If that sounds gross to you, all I can say is you need to come to Brooklyn and try them—and then, like me, you will dream of them whenever you leave home and can't have them. I hope to someday personally go to China and thank the people there for the best food import, *ever*.

Our roof is not fancy. The floor is basic loose gravel covered by tar paper and a layer of green-friendly eco-tarp. There is a four-foot safety fence all the way around the perimeter. We have three chaise lounges and a wooden coffee table painted sky blue. Mom hides the roof vents with a trellis of beach roses. She comes up here to read, Dad to think, and I come up with my friends to hang out.

"Be careful up there," Mom says as she hands me the brown bag from Sung Chu Mei.

"Ma, I'm *fifteen,*" I remind her, as if she doesn't know, and as if my birthday is not seared on her brain.

"That's why I won't come up to check on you," Mom says, getting those creases between her eyes that tell me she's going to worry no matter how much I reassure her. "Because I trust you." She gathers paper plates, napkins, and chopsticks from the kitchen cabinet. "I think it's nice that you're including Maurice."

"It would be rude not to."

"Still. I'm proud of you."

"I just spent a year at an all-girl school. A little testosterone is nice, if just for observational purposes."

Mom throws her head back and laughs. "I'll tell your father you said that. He will like the idea of observation."

"I live to serve."

Mom goes to the sink to clean up some dishes, and for a second, I want to tell her all about Jared Spencer, not just the little bits she knows, but absolutely everything. I want to tell her about how I met him at Grabeel Sharpe Academy, and how he kissed me and gave me Sidney Lumet's book, and how we went together to Wendy Luck's one-woman show on the Saint Mary's College campus, and how when we were in competition with each other at the film festival, he dumped me because my movie was better. But I don't. If I tell my mother all this, she will worry that I'm way into boys and might end up like Esme Amberg, who fell in love with a boy and ran away from Prefect, never to return. I'm not boy crazy like Esme, I'm just hopeful that someday I will have what I once did with Jared Spencer—when he was a good egg and before he went rotten on me.

"You need something?" Mom turns to face me, wondering what I'm still doing there.

"Nope. Send Caitlin up when she gets here."

I climb the steps to the third floor and then through my parents' bedroom to the roof. I could never do anything against the rules in this house, because everything is connected. All you have to do is stand on the landing and you know everything that's happening on a particular floor. I figure Mrs. Pullapilly knows that or she wouldn't let Caitlin come over *ever.* And nobody wants to hang out at Caitlin's, because it's just too uncomfortable. They serve suspicion over there for snacks.

The roof is truly a sanctuary. I set the take-out bag down on the table, along with the plates and utensils. I go to the street side of the roof and look out over the fence. The streets below are summer busy, lots of visitors and neighbors out to shop. I can hear thumps of bass lines coming from cars, and the occasional cacophony of horns, and more than one "*Yo.*"

I look out over the neighborhood and see other rooftop gardens. Some are flat and plain, with only an air-conditioning unit and some old pots as decoration, and others are way too fancy, as if they were inspired by terraces on a palace overlooking a kingdom other than Bay Ridge.

The Melfis have an awning with tassels, while the Hounsells have a fountain next to a picnic table. There are all sorts of ways to "roof it." The Chesterton roof is serviceable and plain, just like we like it.

"Hal-lo," Maurice says from the porthole to the roof.

"Come on up," I tell him.

He climbs up onto the roof and walks over to the fence. "This is an amazing view. So many buildings."

"By the end of the summer, you will know them all, and who's living in them," I tell him.

"I doubt that. I'm not very good with names."

"I'm Viola."

He laughs. "I can remember that."

"And . . . ," I continue, "we say More-*reece* in the states, but in the UK, you are Morris."

"Brilliant," Maurice says, meaning the opposite of brilliant.

I'm boring our tenant to death already. And let's face it, anything he says with that British accent sounds way smarter than anything I say with my American one. "Now, don't make fun of your host. Sarcastic doesn't play on the roof in Brooklyn."

Maurice sort of exhales, like I'm all right after all.

Suzanne taught me that boys are very simple to understand when it comes to girls. If a boy talks to you at all, he probably likes you. Girls are not that way, in my experience. We'll talk to anybody, and it doesn't have to wind up as a date.

I take a good long look at Maurice as he surveys my neighborhood, and decide, right now, in this moment, that he could be a *friend*, but not a *boyfriend*. I am not compelled by him as I was by Jared Spencer, and I'm not instantly comfortable with him as I was with Andrew when we were little in Mommy, Music, & Me classes at Chelsea Day School, and then every day since. I exhale in relief. I let go of that uncomfortable tension that comes with unmet expectations. Instead, I will demonstrate a genuine interest in him and his opinions. "So, what do you think of New York so far?"

"I rather like it."

"You've only seen the airport and Brooklyn."

"Everyone has seen Manhattan, whether they have ever set foot on the island or not. Think about it. So many movies made with New York as a backdrop. It's almost as if there's no need to visit, because you know it already."

"Good point." I'm impressed that he thinks things through so thoroughly. That has not been my experience with boys in general. Even Jared Spencer needed the occasional reminder that he wasn't the only person on the planet. "Well, you know, the same is true of London. There's Big Ben and the Thames, and Buckingham Palace. I've never been to London, and I feel like I have."

"There's so much more to it. Places like Brick Lane. . . ." Maurice's voice trails off. I think the excitement of landing has worn off and now he's homesick.

"What's so special about Brick Lane?" I ask.

"My friends."

"Hi!" Caitlin says as she climbs through the porthole onto the roof. "Your mom sent me with the drinks." She hauls our mini-cooler up. Maurice turns at the sound of her voice. "I put my duffel in your room."

As Caitlin emerges from the landing, she appears like a goddess in a myth, coming out of the earth. Her long hair is ruffled by the wind like shiny strands of black licorice. Her baby blue T-shirt is piped in white ribbon, while her jeans have rhinestone studs on the pockets. Caitlin, though she is Indian, is a lot like the Italian girls in my neighborhood. Exotic brunettes like a little dazzle in their wardrobe.

Maurice, who was perfectly normal ten seconds ago, suddenly goes all shy as Caitlin approaches.

"Caitlin, say hello to Maurice from England." I turn to Maurice.

"Nice to meet you." Caitlin smiles.

I swear, it's like Maurice can't handle her smile. He's turning ten shades of red.

"Are you hungry?" I ask Caitlin.

"Starving."

"How about you?" I ask Maurice.

"I am."

"Well, make yourselves at home. We've got sesame noodles, vegetable dumplings, and sautéed green beans."

"Sounds delish," Caitlin says.

"You guys have no idea. Well, Maurice, we've just met, but I had to spend last school year in a boarding school, and of course, I missed my friends, but second on the list of things I learned I could not live without was . . . cold sesame noodles."

"I understand." He smiles and sits on one of the chaise lounges. "I miss my mother's shortbread."

Caitlin helps me unload the take-out from the bag.

"What's your favorite food, Maurice?" Caitlin asks. "Besides your mom's baking."

"Indian."

She laughs. "You're just saying that to be polite."

"No, I'm not. My favorite food is kuttu ki puri," he says.

"What's that?" I ask.

"My mom makes them." Caitlin beams. "They're puffy potato balls fried in oil."

"In London, they are filled with different things," Maurice explains, scooting the edge of his chaise closer to Caitlin's.

"Little bundles of savories—like vegetables, or sometimes mixtures of meat and spices," Caitlin says.

"I like the vegetables best," he says.

"Me too," she agrees.

Then the craziest thing happens. It's as if I, the host of the evening, have evaporated like a bubble into thin air and am floating above the roof and over Bay Ridge into the harbor. Maurice is over his shyness, and Caitlin revels in his knowledge of her Indian culture. They *like* each other.

I can't wait to IM Suzanne and tell her that her theories about boys need a redo, because Maurice was totally comfortable with me from the start, while he was shy/nervous/longing with Caitlin. He has, in fact, already totally fallen for Caitlin, who made his throat close with nerves, and not for me, whom he could talk easily with.

Cupid dropped a love bomb over Bay Ridge, and these two are sucking fumes. Even Jared Spencer and I had a slight warm-up period, where I wasn't sure if it was me or my camera he was interested in. But these two? They found common ground over Indian cuisine with the fried potato puffs, whatever they are, and they haven't stopped talking since.

A sliver of a periwinkle moon appears through a dusting of clouds. It lingers over us like a shard of pretty ribbon. I don't think Caitlin and Maurice notice that the sun has set, that they haven't eaten, or that I'm here. I turn on the old string of bulbs that light the roof. They don't even notice the twinkle. This is how it goes, I'm thinking, when you meet The One.

* * *

"Is it too hot in here?" I ask Caitlin.

"Not at all." She lies back on the pillow inside her sleeping bag, while I, feeling the heat, lie on the outside of mine.

"So what did you think of Maurice?" I ask her.

There's a long pause, and then we both start laughing so hard, I'm afraid it might wake my parents.

"He must be deported immediately," Caitlin jokes.

"I'll call the authorities in the morning." I play along.

"He's wonderful." Caitlin turns over and props her face on her hand.

"But you think everybody is wonderful," I tell her.

Caitlin nods. She knows it's true. "What can I say? I see the good in everybody."

"So what's so great about Maurice?"

Caitlin takes a deep breath. "He has beautiful green eyes."

"They're green, all right," I agree.

"And he knows a lot about Indian culture. I feel like he totally understands me." Caitlin lies back down on her pillow. She is quiet for a long time.

"What's the matter?"

"He leaves on August thirtieth. That doesn't give us much time," she says sadly.

When I was at boarding school, in the beginning,

when I really and truly hated it, I took out a calendar and counted the days I had to be there—it was 142 days total, and it might as well have been a million. Time passes slowly when you're miserable, and so fast when you want it to stay. I know this from experience. "Caitlin, instead of getting all sad about it, why don't you just have fun?"

"I guess."

"Maybe you'll hate his guts by Friday. You never know."

"True. But I doubt it."

"You don't have to figure everything out tonight."

The whirl of the old fan drones in the dark. Caitlin goes off to sleep with dreams of the green-eyed boy from London. I remember Jared Spencer and how I felt the first time I met him at the dance at Grabeel Sharpe—and how my stomach was doing flip-flops at the thought of him. I halfway think that's the best part of love, the beginning. But it doesn't matter now; Jared Spencer is so far away, he might as well be a dream.

FOUR

"WHAT'S WRONG?" ANDREW OPENS THE DOOR TO the Bozellis' apartment in Cobble Hill. It's a large loft that used to be a bakery. It is big and plain, with lots of floor space, built for boys. It always smells like popcorn, and there's a pile of men's and boys' beat-up, ratty tennis shoes by the door. Four guys add up to a lot of shoes.

The only proof that Mrs. Bozelli lives here is the fancy umbrella stand with a drawing of a woman in the rain on it. It's just about the only feminine touch in the whole place. I barge right in and throw down my purse. This loft is like my second home, but it's changed since I went to boarding school.

"Nice." I look around. The Bozellis painted the living room bright red and added big, soft, overstuffed chairs and a sofa, covered in white washable canvas slipcovers.

"Mom said she couldn't take it anymore. She needed a change. All of a sudden she wants nice things, now that we're all teenagers."

"Can't blame her."

"You want a soda?"

"Sure." I sit down on the washable slipcovers and can actually smell the bleach. "How were your cousins?"

"They have a sailboat. We went out on Long Island Sound."

"Sounds fun."

"Not really. My uncle Bill assigns everybody a job. It's not like you can sit and enjoy the view. I was in charge of wrapping these giant ropes that secure the sail. And then, when you're sailing, you have to keep adjusting them or the thing will tip over." Andrew looks at me. "Okay, so tell me what's going on."

"Caitlin and Maurice are over at my house right now with my mom. Maurice is teaching Mom how to make scones for proper tea."

"That's cool."

"Caitlin told her mom that she's with me."

Andrew thinks for a moment. "You realize this will never work." Andrew pulls a cold bottle of Stewart's cream soda (my fave) from the fridge and hands it to me.

"I know I said I didn't have a job this summer—but now I do. I'm in the unpaid position of keeping Caitlin and Maurice's dates a secret."

"I wouldn't worry about it. They'll probably break up before Mrs. Pullapilly finds out about it. Anything that happens this fast is doomed to failure. Maurice is only here till the end of summer."

"Doesn't matter. Time is not an obstacle for true love. We were on the roof, and I swear when they looked at each other, it cued the doves to start cooing. This is for real. They're soul mates."

"That's something girls made up to make guys stick around."

"I'm mildly insulted." I take a swig of my soda.

"Olivia used to say that we were soul mates. First of all, my soul doesn't have a mate, nor can it date. I kind of resented it every time she said it. It didn't make me feel good, it freaked me out—like there was some other parallel universe involved in having a girlfriend and going out for pizza and going to movies."

"That might be true for you. But it's not for Caitlin. I'm telling you, it was like that mysterious marshmallow-scented steam that comes up out of the manholes that nobody can quite figure out—like a fog came up the side of our building and drugged them."

Andrew says, "Wait and see how it plays out."

I can always tell when Andrew is done with a topic. "You want to go to the Village?"

"If we don't go shopping."

"We can go over to Hudson River Park."

"Great."

Andrew grabs his keys. He texts his mom and I text mine to tell them our plans. One of the best things about having a lifelong BFFAA in Andrew is that my parents don't freak out when I want to go somewhere with a boy. I don't know what I'd do if I were Caitlin. I don't know what I'd do if my parents were suspicious of me and my friends. I hope I never have to find out.

Here's the crazy thing about our new British tenants: They totally fit in. I don't mind Maurice showing up for breakfast, and my parents like it when Mr. Longfellow stops by for a glass of wine after rehearsal. Mom breaks out the Italian cheeses and salami. They sit around and talk about all kinds of stuff, while Maurice and I hang out in the living room texting our friends.

Mom has become an expert scone maker. She even went to Cobble Hill and picked up special tea and jams. Maurice feels bad that Mom goes to so much trouble. He said all he needs is a pot of tea and a biscuit or two, nothing fancy. (Biscuits are cookies.) But Mom loves a culinary challenge, not to mention anything that expands her international horizons, so for now, she's into proper tea for our temporary guests.

I've learned a few things about tea since the Longfellows moved in. Never squeeze the tea bag into the cup; it turns the tea bitter. There's no fancy way to make tea. Maurice makes the tea in Mom's old pot with plain old bags of English Breakfast and boiling water. Lemon and honey are better choices than milk and sugar.

"Hi, guys." Caitlin comes into the kitchen with a bag from the grocery store. "Clotted cream for you, Mrs. Chesterton."

"Thanks, Caitlin." Mom puts on her oven mitts and takes the baking pan of scones out of the oven. Maurice smiles at Caitlin, and she smiles back. I fade into the wallpaper like a cabbage rose in the pattern.

"You know, I'd love to invite your mom over for tea sometime." Mom slides the puffy scones off the tray with a spatula and onto one of the platters from Grand's wedding china (first marriage).

"She's very busy," Caitlin says quietly. "With her job."

"Is she going to take any time off this summer?"

"We go to Woodstock and rent a house for two weeks when Dad takes off."

“How nice.” Mom spoons the jam into a small bowl.

Mom’s invitation for Mrs. Pullapilly to join us was like a sudden storm cloud covering the sun and turning the afternoon dark as night. Maurice, who knows by now that there are rules regarding Caitlin, busies himself pouring tea, as I gather the sugar and cream.

“It’ll just be us for now,” I chirp, hoping to break the mood. I slather the clotted cream on the scone and take a bite. “Mom, let’s move to England!”

Caitlin and Maurice laugh, and for a moment, we aren’t thinking about anything but scones; we’re just having fun.

I give Maurice a MetroCard. The sooner he’s comfortable getting around on the subway, the better. He will need to meet his dad after rehearsal (it’s not held in the theater in which the play will run), and I don’t want to spend the summer taking Maurice everywhere he needs to go. I give him a map. “So you take the Q to Times Square. And then you go to the rehearsal space at Forty-fifth Street and Ninth Avenue.”

“I got it.” He turns to Caitlin. “See you tomorrow?”

“Sure.”

Caitlin watches Maurice go down the stairs to the subway.

"I'll walk you home," I tell her. "Are you going to tell your mom about Maurice?"

"He's only here for the summer."

"Good point."

"I mean, if he went to LaGuardia and I felt like this, I might have to tell her. But Maurice will only be here until the end of August, and I think it's best if I don't say anything."

"Whatever you want to do is fine with me," I tell her.

And then, for the rest of the ten-block walk, we don't say a word. In all the years I've been friends with Caitlin, we never ran out of things to say. But today is different. Please don't let Caitlin be one of those girls who changes when she likes a boy. I don't think I could take it.

In honor of the old days, when Andrew and I would make movies about whatever random subjects we liked, we've decided to take our cameras to Coney Island to make a short documentary about Mermaid Day. A regular trip to Coney Island on any summer day is always fun, but on Mermaid Day, it's an *experience*.

MD truly is, next to Christmas, my favorite annual holiday.

Every third Saturday in June since anyone can remember, mermaids have invaded the boardwalk on

Coney Island and held a parade. It's the official kickoff for the summer beach season.

Mortals, women dressed up as mermaids, come from everywhere to honor the goddesses of the sea. They are swathed in gold lamé, wear serpentine wigs with sprayed curls, and every single one has a version of a tail fin as part of her costume. They paint their faces in sea colors and wear wild net headdresses and drippy earrings and necklaces made of heaps of pearls and branches of coral.

The mermaids are all ages, from babies to grandmothers. There are even families of mermaids. Mothers push their babies in strollers, swaddled in sequined costumes. They promenade down the boardwalk to island music, lifting their dazzling fins held up by invisible wires. It is street theater.

Crowds of onlookers, including my friends and me, come from all the boroughs to watch the parade. There are floats with mermaids nestled in giant seashells, and tableaus of mythic sea gods brought to life.

It's a filmmaker's dream, color *and* story in one fabulous parade. After the parade is done, a queen is crowned, then the boardwalk turns into a carnival. We eat pierogis, play games, and wait on long, long lines to go on the ancient wooden roller coaster, aka the Cyclone. If you're lucky, you get to share your seat with a mermaid.

Andrew, Caitlin, Maurice, and I take the Q train from our stop to Stillwell Avenue. It is packed, standing room only. Andrew and I stand and grip the metal poles for balance, as our video cameras in their cases hang safely around our necks. Maurice stands next to Caitlin, whom he scored a seat for. I am not surprised. Maurice has the best manners on earth, and not just because he's British. He's been raised well, Grand says. He is a total gentleman and he treats Caitlin delicately—like a fine bone china teacup.

"Yo, scootch over." An old Italian man in a linen jacket gives Maurice the elbow, then grabs the bar over the seats.

"Pardon me?" Maurice says to the man.

"I said, yo, scootch over. I need some space here."

"Oh yes, right, right," Maurice says, making room for the man.

The crowded train is a challenge for genteel Maurice. Proper English manners don't exist on the Q. Maurice is being poked and shoved, and the passengers never say *excuse me*. Maurice is experiencing the end of civility with one ride to Coney Island.

Maurice is the kind of boy who behaves a certain way to impress a girl. When the train stopped and the doors opened, Maurice boarded the train first, surveyed it, and found a seat for Caitlin. He asked a lady to move her shopping bag to make room for Caitlin. I think the British accent threw her, so she moved the bag quickly. Americans still take orders from the Brits, at least when it comes to seat hogging.

Andrew can't believe that Caitlin and Maurice are an item. It's only been a few days, and no way Andrew believes in love at first sight. He told me he thought that it was impossible to know you like someone after one night of take-out and talking, and a few afternoon teas with scones. Sometimes Andrew is way too practical for his own good.

The train shakes from side to side as it takes a curve. I am thrown up against Andrew. He grabs me before I fall and steadies me. "You've gotta get your sea legs back."

"You got that right." I haven't ridden the subway for a year, and I've totally lost my sense of balance and technique. I used to be able to ride the curves and bumps like a surfer, without holding the bar. Now I grip it with both hands. I don't remember the train being so loud, either.

Maurice takes Caitlin's hand. Andrew looks at them, and then he looks at me. I shrug. No law against hand holding when you're fifteen and riding the Q.

"Have you heard from that guy?" Andrew asks.

"What guy?"

"You know." Andrew looks out the window to the

dark walls of the train tunnel. Oh, I get it; he sees Maurice and Caitlin holding hands and it reminded him of all my emails about Jared Spencer. "That guy from the military academy."

"Jared Spencer."

"Yeah."

"He sent out a group email to all of his friends to tell them that he was going hiking in the Grand Canyon for summer vacation. No personal note or anything. I was part of the bundle."

"Nice." Andrew rolls his eyes.

"That's what I thought. I'm pretty special, aren't I?"

"He's an idiot."

"Not totally." After all, I did date Jared for a whole semester and through one entire Christmas break. We shared a total of eight kisses, six hand holdings, two tickets to a one-woman theater show, and one holiday gift exchange. He was a good boyfriend until the Midwest Secondary School Film Competition, where he went all weird on me. But all in all, as far as boys, conversation, compliments, and mutual interests go, he was actually okay.

"Don't defend him." Andrew's eyes go squinty, and he gets a look on his face that he gets whenever he's annoyed. It's the same expression he'd get when we were six and a mean kid would come along and smash his sand castle at the playground in Prospect Park or when a kid did the same thing to me. No friend is more loyal than Andrew Bozelli. "You deserve better than Jared Spencer. That guy was rude to you."

"Don't worry about me. I *get* boys. Totally." At least I did when Suzanne Santry was around. Now? Not so sure.

"You *think* you do." Andrew smiles.

"Hey, I'm a matchmaker. Look at my handiwork."

Caitlin whispers in Maurice's ear. He laughs.

"And this was tough—an international hook-up," I tell him.

Maurice and Caitlin talk nonstop, utterly fascinated with each other. Talk about a connection. They remind me of a story Marisol gave me to read at Prefect about a couple of monks, who lived in silence and saved up their words for ten years, and finally, when they got a chance to talk again, they couldn't stop. Caitlin was never this chatty, she was more the listening type, but Maurice has changed all that.

"Okay, maybe you're smart about *other* people. But when it comes down to you, you don't get it. That guy Jared was jealous of you."

"I broke up with him. So now he doesn't have a reason to be jealous."

"Here's the deal. You're a better filmmaker than he is, so he used you to make himself better."

"Oh, like Olivia Olson didn't totally control you?" I snark.

Andrew's face flushes red with embarrassment.

"Olivia overhauled everything about you. You even wear Americana jeans now. What happened to the Gap?"

"It's still there," he grumbles.

"Don't get me wrong, you look good."

Andrew smiles at the compliment.

"She did a good job. Olivia is a great boyfriend stylist."

The door opens onto the crowded platform at Stillwell Avenue. Mermaid Day really brings out the crowds. I holler to Caitlin to hang on to Maurice, but no worries, they are still holding hands. I give Andrew a nudge so he checks out the hand holding. He raises his eyebrows but doesn't say a word. We work our way through the crowds from the platform to the boardwalk. I lift my camera out of the case, flip the lens cap, and begin to film the pre-parade chaos.

I stand in the center of the throng as they move toward the boardwalk. I hold up my camera and do a 360 of the crowd, an improvised over-the-head shot, with a steady hand. A father with his three-year-old daughter dressed as a mermaid in a pink sequined costume with gold net fins pushes through.

"Mermaid on board," he shouts.

I go in for a close-up of the little girl. She grins for the camera. I flip the shutter speed to slow and film her in midair as she perches on her dad's shoulders against the pristine blue sky.

"Nice shot," Andrew says.

"Thanks."

Andrew leads us to the edge of the boardwalk. We push to the front to get a good view of the mermaid parade. "You get the walkers, I'll get the floats. Okay?" Andrew asks.

"Great."

"We'll edit it all together later."

"Have you made a movie together before?" Maurice asks.

"Sometimes." Andrew shrugs.

"Viola keeps a video diary too. She has since she was a little girl," Caitlin says proudly. "She made a short-subject movie already. It won an award in the Midwest."

"You should show my father sometime. He would like to see your work," Maurice says.

"Violet Riot!" I turn toward the parade route. Coming down the boardwalk, where the procession of mermaids will be, is Tag Nachmanoff, the handsomest guy in Brooklyn, and my personal ideal/crush. He looks *amazing*. He has grown his black hair long. He wears black aviator sunglasses, and boot-leg jeans with a black T-shirt that says METROPOLITAN MUSEUM OF ART in tiny white letters. His black Converse sneakers have no laces. He is hanging with three other guys, but he walks a few steps ahead of them. He comes over to us, smiling that wide, perfect smile.

"Hi, Tag." I am so glad I wore my boho blouse with the flowy sleeves and a pleated skirt. I'm wearing my best not-too-casual outfit and now, in a split second, it's not wasted.

"You grew up." He smiles at me.

"I had to. I was a pioneer girl in Indiana for a whole year."

"I heard."

"Thanks for your email."

"Anytime." Tag nods. I swear his hair swings in slow motion.

Caitlin and Andrew say hello to Tag. Andrew is way less impressed, but that's because he thinks that Tag is a *player*—that way too many girls are after him, which makes him suspect and not legit. Andrew got to see Tag in action at LaGuardia last year, and he didn't always like what he saw. Of course, I got an email from Andrew giving me the details. Tag can come off as cocky, while Andrew is anti-ego. Of course, it doesn't help that Andrew knows I'm practically obsessed with Tag and have been since I first saw him.

I was thirteen at Chelsea Piers, taking ice skating lessons. Tag, who is older, was on a junior hockey league. One day, when class was over, the teacher asked me to take a run around the rink in my skates so she could check my form. So I did. And out there alone on the ice, I started to move faster and faster. When I spun around the far lip of the rink, I saw Tag standing at the gate, waiting to come onto the ice. I was so entranced by him, I didn't slow down enough and had to go up on my toes when I got to the gate. Tag saw what was happening and came out and grabbed me before I hit the wall. He didn't save my life, but he saved my face. Tag made it look like we were ice dancers—for thirty seconds.

"Tag, this is Maurice. He's here for the summer from London. His dad is directing a Broadway show."

"All right." Tag nods his head, impressed. "I do a little acting."

"Tag was in a Dollar Store commercial," I explain. "It's on YouTube."

"I can't imagine who put it there," Andrew says innocently.

Tag shrugs. "Probably somebody who likes commercials."

"Probably." Andrew fiddles with the lens cap on his camera.

"Are you gonna film the parade, Drewmeister?" Tag says to Andrew. Andrew has never been called Andy or Drew, or anything meister; in fact, he hates nicknames.

"Yeah."

"You home all summer?" Tag looks at me.

"Yep, and very happy about it."

Tag smiles. "Well, I'm around," he says.

"Great." I smile back at him.

"See you around," Tag says. He walks down the boardwalk like he owns it, and nobody stops him, not a handler from the parade or a policeman on the beat. Tag N. can go anywhere he pleases. It's his world. Everybody notices him. And I can't believe it, he noticed *me*, and not only did he find me in this huge crowd, he made a point to come over and talk to me. This day officially could not get any better.

"Tag is an interesting name. I know Tads, but no Tags," Maurice says.

"Viola is in love with him," Andrew says.

"I am not."

"He's your crush."

"Well, I don't go around announcing it." It's true. I

don't. And Andrew, as my BFFAA, should know not to *out* my desire for Tag in public. I would *never* embarrass him.

"Sorry," Andrew says. And this is why he will always be my best friend. If he does slip up, he acknowledges it immediately. This is the sign of a mature person.

I am *not* as mature as Andrew.

A small island combo playing kettle drums works its way down the boardwalk. People take out their phones and commence taking pictures. Mermaids pour onto the ramp of the boardwalk. The costumes are stunning: Tinfoil gills shimmer, blue glittery silk capes flow, emerald green ruffles of fins drape onto the ground. The parade is a rainbow of mermaids. I keep the shot steady on the walking mermaids when I see Olivia Olson in the background of my shot.

"Andrew. Olivia's here." I point the camera in her direction.

Andrew looks over his shoulder toward her.

Olivia Olson is truly gorgeous in that lucky born-that-way fashion. Her blond hair hangs straight in streaks of champagne gold. No frizz, and I bet it doesn't take her nine months to grow out bad bangs. She wears white shorts and a black T-shirt and gold strappy platform sandals. She is popular. Her posse, girls from LaGuardia who are into fashion as art and plan on college at FIT in three years, flutter around her like butterflies. Olivia has it *all*. Suddenly, my boho blouse seems too billowy, and my skirt is wrinkled. Not a good look when comparing myself to a goddess.

Olivia checks her BlackBerry, and then goes up on her toes and waves down the boardwalk. Tag checks his BlackBerry, turning in her direction. He slips the BlackBerry into his pocket and heads back toward Olivia.

Andrew has pushed his way to the edge of the crowd and is filming a float of pink net jellyfish made with bubble wrap. He officially ignores Olivia, while I am engrossed by the scene as it unfolds.

When Tag reaches Olivia, he gives her a big hug. She kisses him on the cheek. A ripple of pea green jealousy peels through me, or maybe it's just the heat from the bright sun. Andrew checks his shot in the playback. Then he looks up. He sees Olivia and Tag across the boardwalk. Caitlin leans over and whispers, "Do you believe it? Tag and Olivia?"

"Yeah." I tell her. And I do. Of course Olivia and Tag found each other at LaGuardia High School. Once Olivia made over Andrew, she needed a new challenge. It's as if she was done with Andrew after his braces came off, because once his bite was corrected he had achieved his maximum potential. Olivia likes makeovers as much as I enjoy editing film. It's her talent. I don't know what she's going to find wrong with Tag, but if there is a flaw, Olivia will find it and fix it.

But even with the new haircut, wardrobe, and braces off, Andrew is a film geek. He is simply a better-looking version of his old self, which I always believed was absolutely fine and had its own merits.

And me? I may have grown my bangs out, found my personal style, turned fifteen, had my first boyfriend, and survived the breakup, but to Tag Nachmanoff, I'll always be *Violet Riot*, the girl who understands the Avid and is handy with computers. I will never be Olivia Olson, LaGuardia goddess.

Andrew catches Olivia's eye. He waves at her and smiles cordially. She waves back.

"Let's get the island band," he says.

Olivia doesn't ruffle Andrew *at all*. Zero drama. He is not jealous of Tag one bit. Despite his initial surprise, he waved at his ex like she was any friend, on any day, on any boardwalk. I love this about Andrew. He does *not* obsess. He does *not* hold on to the things that hurt him. He lets it go. I can't say I would be the same if Jared Spencer were across the boardwalk with Olivia Olson. If it were me, I'd probably have a nervous breakdown, turn off my camera, and get back on the Q train and cry eleven stops till I got home. Not Andrew. He's more concerned about getting some great images on film. This is why he is my BFFAA—he's a good example to me in all things. We look at life through the same lens.

"I'm starving," Andrew says.

"I'd like a slice of pepperoni pizza," I tell him. "You guys want to get pizza?" I ask Caitlin and Maurice.

"We had cotton candy. If it's okay, I'd rather show Maurice the boardwalk and then we can walk on the beach," Caitlin says.

"I can see Caitlin home later," Maurice says. "To your house."

Of course he won't see her home to the Pullapillys' apartment; Mrs. P would have a stroke. "You don't want to ride back with us?"

Caitlin and Maurice look at each other. "We'll be fine," Caitlin says.

"Okay." I shrug.

Maurice and Caitlin head down the boardwalk. Andrew changes out the lens on the camera. "Don't make a big deal out of it, Vi," he says.

Too late for that, I'm thinking.

* * *

"Oh, Viola, you didn't reapply your sunblock," my mom says as I bolt through the kitchen.

"No biggie." I put down my camera on the kitchen table.

"How were the mermaids?"

"Andrew and I got the entire parade."

"I like the seashell."

I got my face painted, a tasteful seashell on my cheek. "Thanks! Caitlin got a seahorse."

"Dinner at seven. Grand called. She's got a job offer for you. Give her a call." Mom hands me the phone. I guess it's time for me to join the work world. It feels like I'm the last fifteen-year-old in Brooklyn without a summer job. I press speed dial.

"Hey, Grand. Mom says you have a summer job for me."

"Cleo needs a dog walker."

I think for a moment. This wasn't exactly the summer project I was hoping for, but cash is cash. "Okay."

"I'll pay you ten dollars a day. She has to be walked at lunchtime."

"Sounds good."

"Now, you know, this doesn't count for your summer project. We still have to come up with something exciting and educational."

"I'm making a doc with Andrew about Mermaid Day."

"That's a start. But I'm thinking of something to really make you stretch."

I hang up the phone. Grand is going to come up with something weird like working on a loom making rugs, hemming draperies, or making scented soap on her roof terrace. My summer project, whatever it is, will involve making something useful. Great.

I check the clock. "Mom, I've got to Skype." I climb the back stairs. I race into my room and flip open my laptop. Suzanne has coordinated a group Skype from her mom's office with Marisol, Romy, and me. It will be like being back in the quad at Prefect, except this time, we're onscreen in cyberspace.

I type the Skype number. It dials through to Mrs. Santry's line. Suddenly, Suzanne's face appears.

"Hi, Suz!"

"Whoa. Let me drop the volume. I'm in Mom's office, and everything in here is on blare." Suzanne smiles. Her honey-colored hair is pushed back with a hair band. "Cool face painting."

"Thanks!" I say loudly.

"Lower your volume."

"Too loud? Sorry."

"Hey, guys." Romy's face appears in a square next to Suzanne.

"Romy!" Suzanne and I say together. Romy is already tan, no doubt from living on the hockey field since she got to camp. She talked her coach into letting her use the computer in the athletic office for our Skype.

"This camp is the best. I got selected for the first team. I'm a guard."

"All those hours of practice at Prefect paid off," I tell her.

"How's it going there?" Romy asks me.

"Too much to tell you."

"I like the face painting," Romy says.

I touch my face unconsciously, already forgetting that I had a seashell painted on my cheek and across my chin. "Big news. Tag Nachmanoff showed up."

"Did he notice you?" Romy asks.

"Hey, everybody!" Marisol waves from a square beneath Romy.

"Good, you're here. I don't have to repeat the big story of the day."

"Tell all." Marisol leans in.

"Tag Nachmanoff is still the most gorgeous guy ever. Remember Olivia, Andrew's girlfriend? Well, it turns out after she dumped Andrew, she went for Tag."

"Poor Andrew," Marisol says.

"No, he's totally cool. And he looks cute without his

braces. No worries. He's fine."

"I *knew* Andrew would blossom into a hottie," Marisol says.

"Insane. Isn't it? How about you?"

"No summer crush for me. I'm working at Target. I'm in the home and garden section, but I have to help out front. I walk, like, a billion miles a day. And I hate the apron. But I get a discount! I got the entire mini eyeshadow collection from Boots."

"I had a date," Suzanne announces. "But there will *not* be a second one."

"What happened?" Romy asks.

"It was weird. I knew Lucas through my brother Kevin. . . ."

"Update, please!" Romy begs. "I'm fifteen now. Tell him!" Romy still has a crush on the totally unattainable Kevin Santry—he's twenty, but he's as handsome as Tag N., Midwest version.

"My brother is still dating Maeve from Ireland. Sorry, Romy."

"Ah well." Romy sighs.

"Go back to your date, Suz," Marisol says.

"Well, we go out to eat at the food court at Fenway Mall. Normal. He is nice, cute. I like him a lot so far. And then, he started talking about his ex-girlfriend. She sounds really great and I said, you should call her."

"You told your date to go back to his ex?" Marisol marvels.

"He still likes her. So why not?"

This is one of the things I love about Suzanne. She's nonchalant about her studies, her looks, and boys. It's really something to aspire to—and it makes me miss her more. "So what's the word in NYC?" Suzanne asks.

"Well, Grand is going to be in a Broadway show. *Arsenic and Old Lace* is moving. And they got a big director from England. It opens in six weeks."

"That's so exciting!" Marisol says.

"How cool," Romy says.

"Your grand must be stoked," Suzanne says.

"Totally. This is really big. She hasn't been on Broadway for years. And her boyfriend, George, is in it too."

"He's my ideal man," Marisol says wistfully.

"I've never seen a Broadway show," Romy says.

"Bus-and-truck at the Goodman—that's all I've seen," Suzanne says.

"We could never afford it," Marisol says.

"Hey, why don't you guys come for opening night? Grand gets some free tickets—and you could stay here. I could show you New York."

"But how would we get there?" Marisol says.

"You could take the train from Charlottesville," I suggest. Marisol and I Googled the distance between Richmond, Virginia, and New York City at Prefect before school ended, because we could not bear the thought that we would never see each other again. We checked out the Amtrak schedule. And we figured, maybe Marisol could visit, in case by some miracle, the Carreras family hit the lottery and Marisol could afford to come to New York.

"I could save up," Marisol says. "I do have a job."

"Guys, I don't mean to be a downer, but I really don't want to leave Chicago this summer."

"Your dad?" Marisol asks.

"Yeah, he's not doing so great," Suzanne says sadly. "I just want to spend every moment with him."

"Maybe he'll get a little better and we can revisit the plan," Romy offers.

"You never know." Suzanne smiles.

"Okay, then let's think about it. New York City in August."

Once I sign off Skype, Andrew IM's me.

AB: ***How was the Skype?***

Me: Girls are great. I asked them to come to New York.

AB: ***That would be fun.***

Me: Sorry about Olivia today.

I wait for Andrew's reply. Weird. He doesn't reply. So I type.

Me: I said, I'm sorry about Olivia today.

AB: *I'm not.*

Me: But you acted cool.

For a moment I feel bad that I brought this up.

AB: *I was surprised. How about Tag?*

Me: He likes whoever's hot, not whoever's interesting. I'm *out*.

AB: *He said he was around.*

Me: I have better ways to spend my summer.

AB: *Good answer.*

Sometimes I wonder if Andrew thinks I'm ever so slightly shallow. I've hung on to the Nachmanoff dream for years now. Maybe he thinks the crush has worn out its welcome and it's time for me to stop mooning for the guy I'll never have.

AB: *When do you want to cut the parade footage?*

Me: We better do it before you leave for camp.

AB: *My house or yours?*

Me: Mine. Less noise.

AB: *Right.*

Me: Caitlin is not going to tell her mom about Maurice.

AB: *Bad idea.*

Me: I know. But what can I do?

AB: ***If her mother finds out, she'll blame you for corrupting Caitlin.***

Me: I know. I think I'll talk to Mom about it.

AB: *She's cool.*

Me: She'll know what to do.

Andrew signs off. I flip my laptop closed and plug it into the charger. My mother *will* know what to do. I just wish Maurice wasn't so internationally intense. He is so crazy about Caitlin, I don't know if he gets that he can't show it if he ever meets Mrs. Pullapilly. Caitlin and I used to be a lot alike; we idolized boys from afar. She hasn't had a first boyfriend, a Jared Spencer, and then lost him, to put things in perspective.

Caitlin and I founded the Tag Nachmanoff Fan Club, but he was unattainable, so we never had to deal with the possibility that he might ever want to date us. Caitlin also likes movie stars, probably for the exact same reason: She knows she'll never meet one.

I am in the midst of a conundrum.

I want Caitlin to be happy, although she will be

anything *but* if her mother finds out that she has a boyfriend. No matter how wonderful Maurice Longfellow is, he does not fit into Mrs. Pullapilly's plan for Caitlin's future.

Caitlin might get her wish to be in a big drama this summer. I hope it's not the Brooklyn version of *Romeo and Juliet*.

FIVE

THE DOG-WALKING JOB IS GIVING ME A PLACE I HAVE to be every day at noon. So immediately, like Caitlin and my old roommates, I have a job to do and a schedule to keep.

Grand lives in a white-brick high-rise on the East Side of Manhattan at 80th and York, overlooking the East River. I take the subway to her apartment, and take Cleo out while she and George are at rehearsal. Grand wants her mind free to work on the play, and hiring me means she can relax about Cleo. It also means I can hang around and wait for her and George to come home. I like to be with them; they have such interesting jobs and meet fascinating people.

Rehearsals for *Arsenic and Old Lace* are held in a studio

on 45th Street and Ninth Avenue. Play rehearsals don't take place in the theater where the play will run. During rehearsals, there is no set, no lights, no costumes, just tape on the floor to show where the scenery will go. Rehearsals are all about blocking and finding the meaning of the play. When they're not in rehearsal, the actors are kept busy with costume fittings and publicity.

Grand and George love to walk home together after rehearsal, because it gives them a chance to hash through everything the director told them. "I do my best thinking on my feet," Grand says. It is a requirement of all New Yorkers to love walking. Even when you take a train or a bus, you have to get to the station or stop, and then walk to your destination.

Grand swears she is trim and in good health because she walks everywhere. "Never set foot in a gym in my life, and only married one once." (She refers to my former step-granddad Jim.) So Grand didn't need a dog to walk as an excuse to get off the couch, as she was already a confirmed city walker. When she has the time, she has even "pep stepped" down the East Side of Manhattan and over the Brooklyn Bridge to visit us. She considers the Brooklyn Bridge a work of art, and feels part of its majesty when she hikes across it. Usually, we pick her up on the Brooklyn side of the bridge, because we live pretty far from it. Grand is a die-hard New Yorker, through and through. I inherited my love of the city from her.

Grand's apartment is cheery and warm. There are large modern paintings on the walls, including a newly framed poster from the regional theater production of *Arsenic and Old Lace*. She and George are listed in the credits.

Her furniture is comfortable, and some pieces are antiques. She collects odds and ends on her travels, so nothing really matches, but it still looks good altogether. Her terrace is like an extra room. French doors lead to a suite of garden furniture and a small gurgling fountain with a Buddha statue overlooking the East River.

The key turns in the lock. Cleo commences barking.

"Cleo baby!" Grand says. Cleo makes a beeline for Grand and George. George picks her up and nuzzles her as Grand peels off her sunhat and throws her keys into an African basket by the door.

"How'd she do?" George wants to know. I can't help but notice that adults are most concerned about the smallest, whether it is a dog or a child.

"I took her to the dog run on Eighty-sixth. She ruled the park."

"Of course she did. This dog has self-esteem. She put

those weeks in the shelter behind her and found her voice."

"She should run for mayor," I tell Grand.

"Cocktail time," George says. "What'll it be?"

"Iced green tea for me," I say.

"I'll have a gin and tonic," Grand says.

I follow Grand into the kitchen while George fixes our cocktails on the drink cart in the living room. Grand takes several packages of fancy cheeses marked with foil medallions from the fridge and unwraps them.

"What's happening in Brooklyn?" Grand slices the cheese.

"Mom and Dad are cutting their doc."

"How's it going?" Grand places the cheese on a platter and fans the crackers around the edge.

"It's going to be excellent."

"How about your friends?"

"Andrew is getting ready for camp. And Caitlin has fallen for Maurice."

"Can you blame her? He is a handsome young man."

"If her parents find out, they will *kill* her."

"She hasn't told her parents?"

"Are you kidding? They have Caitlin's entire life planned out. And there is no mention of boys anywhere in the conversation, ever."

"Too bad. Relationships are a lovely respite from work. And by fifteen, a young lady should begin navigating those waters."

"I guess." I suppose in my own small way, I have a canoe on those waters already.

"It's appropriate for young ladies to be courted. If a parent forbids that, the young lady will eventually place too much emphasis on boys, and that leads to sneaking, and lying, and all those things we don't want you to do."

"Age-appropriate behavior. That's what Mom calls it."

"Well, she is one hundred percent correct. Take it from me, I learned this the hard way. My parents forbade me to date until I was eighteen, and that was a mistake. I didn't become friends with boys. Friendship is where you learn about someone and what makes them tick. I looked at men like a mystery, and therefore remained in the dark. Until now, that is." She smiles. "The whole trick to boys, or men, as the case may be, is to be a friend first." Grand takes a sip of her drink. "Now tell me, what's troubling you?"

"Caitlin's fallen hard for Maurice. He's totally into her, too. Caitlin uses me as an excuse to see him, because if she told her mom that she liked a boy, she'd never let her come over. I'm afraid it's gonna be

Romeo and Juliet all over again."

"And you're Friar Laurence." Grand puts the pieces together the best way she knows how—by visualizing my friends and me in the cast of a Shakespearean tragedy in which she has performed a featured role sometime in her long career.

"Yeah, the guy who delivers the poison."

"Well, he did pray over them in the final scene, but he was supportive of their love. The friar knew it was real. So you're rooting for Caitlin and Maurice?"

"Why not? She's happy."

"I don't understand why parents forbid these friendships. It's an exercise in futility. Nothing stands in the way of young love, nothing, and especially not hovering parents. Look at Caitlin—she's forced to rebel to follow her heart's desire."

"And she's not even that type."

"No, she isn't. She's a dutiful daughter." Grand picks up the cheese tray. "A pleaser."

I follow Grand out to the terrace. Cleo nips at her heels on the way.

"What a day. What a day." Grand stretches out on the chaise. George serves us our drinks and sits. He extends his long legs on a wicker chair with an ottoman. I perch on a bar stool near the French doors.

"How was rehearsal?" I sip my tea sweetened with wild honey.

"Ask George."

"Well, we've got the play blocked, and now we're off book." George smiles.

"But you already know your lines from the regional production, right?"

"Yes, we do. But in the hands of a new director, we have to listen to his view of the play, and what he envisions. We almost have to let go of the other production entirely."

"Gone. Gone." Grand makes a flourish with her hand.

George laughs. "Les Longfellow is a real thinker. He put the play in a social context of our times."

"Black comedy is big when the stock market is down," Grand says.

"Anyhow, it's like working on an entirely different play," George says.

"Let's talk about you," Grand says. "You should be shadowing someone. After all, what good are connections if we don't use them?"

"Who would walk Cleo?"

"There are hours in between your dog-walking duties. What are you doing in the downtime?"

"Hanging out. Texting."

"A colossal waste of time. Thumb gymnastics. Communication for communication's sake. No, you need a purpose now more than ever, or all you will end up with is nimble fingers on that blueberry."

"BlackBerry," I correct her.

"Whatever. The point is: You need a summer project."

"Do you like the theater, Viola?" George asks.

"Yes, I do. I mean, I'm a filmmaker really. But I know that storytelling began onstage, in front of a live audience. And I know I need to master it, in order to direct movies someday."

"If you had to pick an area of expertise in the theater, any of the skills, which would you choose to master?" George asks.

"You know, when I picked up a camera, my dad taught me that the most important element is the lighting. It makes film art."

"Then you must work with Julius! He's our lighting designer. And an old and dear friend of mine. I'll ask him if you can intern on his crew."

"You would be learning from the best," George says.

Grand's idea fills me with excitement and dread. I'd have to meet a lot of new people, old Broadway hands at that. What will they think of me, a girl who basically knows nothing about what they do? But it's not a bad idea, as I would become a better filmmaker if I learned the technique and use of lighting. It's one thing to shoot on video with ambient light, but it's another entirely to know how to create a mood with instruments. It's eye music really.

Grand grabs her phone and scrolls through until she finds the number she is looking for.

"Julius darling? Yes, it's Coral." She laughs. "I've got a lovely teenage granddaughter who needs grunt work this summer."

She listens.

"She'll do anything," Grand adds. "Excellent." She pauses. "Shall I send her to the brownstone tomorrow?" She listens. "Thank you, Julius. You won't be sorry." Grand hangs up the phone.

"That's done! Your summer project. Now I can rest," Grand says, and she literally, like the great actress she is, indicates the actual behavior of resting and closes her eyes dramatically. Her gin and tonic sweats clear beads in her perfectly manicured, artful long fingers.

George winks at me. "Rest? That'll be the day."

Cleo jumps onto my lap, resting her paws on my thigh. She looks up at me. "Well, Cousin Cleo," I say. "It looks like I have a second job."

* * *

Someday I hope to live in Greenwich Village. Nothing wrong with Brooklyn, but my parents lived in the Village when they were students, long before they were married and before I was born. When the landlord jacked up their rent on 8th Street, and Mom became pregnant with me, they couldn't afford Manhattan anymore, so they moved to Bay Ridge.

Mom and Dad do a lot of maintenance on our building; though the Martinellis took good care of it, there have been many repairs. Mom calls our building an old lady—and she refers to any paint jobs as cosmetic, and any major fix-ups as face-lifts. Our building is like an aging movie star, good bones in need of the occasional fix.

My dream of all dreams is to someday live on Charles Street or West 10th or Bank Street—anywhere in the West Village in Manhattan, below 14th Street. There are lots of cabaret clubs in the Village, and theaters, too—like the Cherry Lane on Commerce Street. NYU and the New School are there too. The streets are shady and wind through the neighborhood like ribbons. I like to film them because the light plays off the bricks, creating a beautiful patina.

I look down at the paper instructing me where to go. Julius Ross lives at 56 Charles Street. The stoop is staggered with terra-cotta pots filled with red geraniums. I ring the bell.

"Who is it?" The voice crackles through the speaker.

"Viola Chesterton. Your intern."

The door buzzes loudly. I push it open and enter the long, dark entryway, brightened up by floor-to-ceiling paintings. A handsome guy in his twenties skips down the stairs toward me. I thought Julius Ross would be ancient. Boy, was I wrong.

"Hello, Mr. Ross," I say politely.

The young man throws his head back and laughs. "I'm Barry. I'm Julius's assistant."

"Oh, sorry. You know, I Googled, but couldn't find a single picture of Mr. Ross."

"That's on purpose. He hates publicity."

"Then why is he in show business?"

Barry laughs louder and longer this time. "Great, Violet."

"Viola."

"Right, right. Like Viola Spolin, the acting teacher."

"Don't know who that is."

"You gonna be a theater major someday?"

"Film."

"Smart girl. No money in the theater."

"Where did you go?"

"I'm in grad school at NYU. This is my penance I'm working off. Come on in. I'll show you the office."

I follow Barry into a living room that is decorated like the stage set of an Agatha Christie mystery. The walls are painted dark blue, the furniture is covered in all shades of blue and mostly in velvet, the draperies have big gold tassels, and the walls are filled with more weird art. A pair of sconces, one in the comedy mask and the other tragedy, are centered over the fireplace. I follow Barry into the back of the brownstone.

"Wow. He has a lot of paintings."

"They're all from sets of plays that he designed the lights for." Barry moves a rolling chair out of his path. "It's kind of a theme with him."

The back room, filled with light, has floor-to-ceiling French doors that open onto a green garden, a mass of tangled vines and shrubs. Buried in the green mess is a statue of Aphrodite, who, weirdly enough, wears a red ski cap. I can't take my eyes off it.

"Harold Prince, the director, put that knit cap on Aphrodite at one of Julius's New Year's parties. Julius swears he'll never take it off." Barry takes a seat behind a desk. A drawing table with a light plot taped to it is angled to get the most light from the doors and windows. The office is cluttered with lots of files, rolls of paper, and squares of gels—cellophane squares placed over lighting instruments to throw different colors. "Okay, your mission, should you choose to take it—"

"I'm here to serve," I remind him.

"—is to run your buns all over New York City. When Julius is in production, he needs stuff from here all the time. So you're gonna spend a lot of time on the subway bringing him stuff."

"No problem."

"He's kind of cranky."

"I can handle it," I promise.

"Okay. Then take this envelope up to Julius. He's at the theater now. They're doing a walk-through. Here's your MetroCard. Let me know when you need another. When you're done, just come back here." Barry sits down at his desk and types on his laptop.

"I have to walk my grandmother's dog at noon."

"Fine. Then after that," he says without looking up. "But get him this envelope now."

"Absolutely." I take the envelope and turn to go. "Uh, Barry?"

"Are you wondering if you get paid?"

"Yeah."

"You'll get a letter of recommendation at the end of

the summer. And if you do a good job, Julius will throw some cash at you."

"Great."

"But don't count on it." Barry grins.

"I won't."

I hop on the A train at West 4th and head to midtown to the theater. I don't know if it's the envelope, or the mission, or the fact that I really am a summer intern for a Broadway lighting designer, but I can't help but smile. Somehow, I feel I'm on my way. Where? Can't say. But somewhere.

The stage door to the Helen Hayes Theatre is propped open with an old can of black deck paint. As I enter the theater, I hear a lot of shouting. I squint in the dark from the side aisle. A man with a gold hoop earring and a bald head is yelling at two other men, who are neither bald nor wearing earrings. They dress more like my dad, in jeans and button-down shirts.

"Julius, we can't spare the first row of the mezz. It's already a small theater. The producers don't want us to remove a single seat."

"They never do! But they don't have to light the thing. I'm supposed to create mood here—instead, it's going to look like the inside of a CVS drugstore. Bright, blue, and blinding . . . tell them they can go and—"

The man with the earring feels my eyes on him. He squints and looks out at me. "Who are you?" he thunders.

"I've got an envelope for Mr. Ross."

"Move it, kid. I haven't got all day."

I practically run to the lip of the stage. Mr. Ross holds out his hand for the envelope as he continues to argue with the men in the oxford shirts. He rips into the envelope as he continues his tirade. When he pulls out the content of the envelope, he gets even angrier. I start to back out of the theater.

"Come here," he growls at me. He fishes in his pocket. "We need coffee." He hands me a twenty-dollar bill.

"How do you like your coffee?"

"Get three black with cream on the side," Mr. Ross growls.

They don't call artists temperamental for nothing.

I find a deli on the corner of 48th and Ninth. I place the coffee order and gather up the little drum creamers and load my pockets with them. I grab napkins and stirrers. I load the black coffee cups into the cardboard carrier, then, juggling them very carefully, head back to the Helen Hayes.

I enter the dark theater, making my way down the

aisle to the stage. I place the coffee on the stage and look around. Mr. Ross and the men are no longer onstage. I take a seat and wait for them. I scroll through my messages. Marisol sent a photo of herself in the garden department of Target, sitting under a giant umbrella holding a decorative frog; Mom sent a reminder of when I have to be home; and Maurice texted for me to cover for Caitlin, as they are taking the Staten Island Ferry to and from lower Manhattan. I text him back to make it a snappy trip. Is it me or are they getting awfully bold, knowing the situation with Caitlin's parents?

I look down at my watch. I've been waiting fifteen minutes by now. I touch the paper coffee cups, which are still warm but beginning to cool. "Mr. Ross?" I call out.

No answer. I call Barry at the office; it goes to voice mail. I leave a message for him to call me back. I put my phone on vibrate and place it on the seat next to me. God forbid it goes off and Mr. Ross hears it.

I settle down into the cool seat in the dark theater and wait.

"Yo, kid."

I open my eyes to a burly old man.

"Don't be afraid. I work here at the theater. I think you fell asleep."

I grab my phone. It's two o'clock! I was supposed to walk Cleo at noon and report back to Barry at the brownstone. The coffee cups are cold and right where I left them. I call my mom. Then I call Grand. No answer. I call Barry at the brownstone. Again, it goes to voice mail.

This is my worst nightmare. I fell asleep in school when I was in the fifth grade, and the teacher let me sleep. I missed the whole day and have been paranoid about napping ever since. I want to cry, but the tears won't come. I just feel that desperation that comes when you know you've missed the party and no one remembered to call you. I race out into the street and grab the crosstown bus to get to Grand's. I get off and run down into the subway to ride uptown.

I run up the subway stairs and out onto 81st Street. I run to Grand's apartment. I wave at the doorman and dash into the elevator. When it opens onto Grand's floor, I search my pockets for the keys, and as I put them in Grand's door, I hear music coming from inside.

"Grand?" I call out.

She pokes her head out of the kitchen. "Oh, hi, Viola." She's annoyed with me.

"I'm so sorry. I fell asleep at the theater waiting for Mr. Ross."

"Cleo had a little accident, but it's okay," Grand says in a tone that says it's far from okay with her.

"I meant to come over at noon." Tears sting my eyes. Doesn't she know that I rushed to get over here at all, once I realized what time it was?

"Viola, when you take on a job, you have to be on time. There really is no excuse."

"I'm sorry," I say again, but the tense expression on Grand's face hasn't left it even with my apology.

"Your mother is expecting you at home. You should go," Grand says frostily.

"I'll be here tomorrow at noon," I promise.

"I hope so," Grand says, and goes back to her kitchen chores.

I cry on and off on the subway all the way home to Brooklyn. Every once in a while, you see a woman crying on the subway and you wonder what could have possibly happened to make her so sad she'd cry in public in front of the other passengers. Now I know. When you're so upset, you don't care. You just weep, stop after blurry stop goes by, people come and people go as the doors open and close, and eventually, you've dried up every last tear, and all that's left is a giant stuffed nose and throbbing headache. I suck at my new intern job, and

Grand is mad at me about the dog walking. I'm a failure in every department, and I just started!

"What happened to you?" Mom asks when I come into the kitchen.

I explain the story and realize, in the telling, that it sounds so lame. But that's me—full of excuses. I sound like an idiot.

"You okay?" Dad asks as he comes in from the hallway lugging groceries. He takes milk from a D'Ag bag and loads it into the fridge.

"She had a rough day. Fell asleep on the intern job."

"Oh boy," Dad says.

"Missed walking Cleo," Mom says.

"Well, when you get a job, you have to set priorities." Dad looks at me. "You're a conscientious girl, Viola. You always have been. I'm sure you'll make it right."

My phone buzzes in my pocket. "Hi, Maurice."

"We're stuck at the pier in Manhattan."

"What do you mean, stuck?"

"The train is out of service. Can you call Mrs. Pullapilly and make up an excuse?"

"You need to get back here."

"Tonight is the concert in Prospect Park. Just tell her that you and Caitlin are going straight there. You can meet us there."

"But I'm not going."

"Would you mind coming along with us tonight?"

This is just great. After the worst day of my summer job life, I have to drag myself to Prospect Park for a free concert and third-wheel status. Nice. "I really need to get some rest so I can do my jobs. . . ."

"Just this once?" Maurice pleads.

"All right, all right." I hang up.

"Everything okay?" Mom asks.

"Just fine," I lie.

Andrew can't come with me to the free concert because his dad has Yankee tickets. Of course there wasn't an extra for me, so now I haven't got an excuse to wiggle out of the concert. I stand on the corner of Prospect Avenue in front of the doughnut shop and wait for Caitlin and Maurice.

After a few minutes, I see them coming toward me.

"We had so much fun on the Staten Island Ferry!" Caitlin smiles. "How was your first day in the theater?"

"Not great."

"Sorry." Caitlin looks at Maurice. If I have a pet peeve, it's when a girl is with a boy and she states an opinion and then looks at the guy for approval.

"We had better hurry—we want to get good seats," Maurice says. I follow them into the crowd at the entrance of the park. "You girls wait here while I get a program."

Caitlin watches Maurice go to the ticket stand.

"Caitlin, I'm worried," I tell her honestly.

"Why?"

"If your mom finds out that you're seeing Maurice . . ."

"But she won't," Caitlin says firmly. "If you don't say anything, who else knows?"

"That's just my point. I don't want to get in trouble. I have enough problems."

"I told my mother that I was staying over with you tonight."

"You can always stay over with me."

"Thanks." Caitlin smiles.

"But you have to tell your mom what's going on. You don't have to make a big deal out of it, just tell her that you like a boy."

"I can't," Caitlin says softly.

"Maybe she'll be nice about it."

"You know my mom."

Maurice returns with the programs. He gives one to Caitlin and one to me. I follow them into the park. Our seats are really just a marked-off area on the grass. Two blue flags indicate where we should sit. I sit down in the grass next to them as a band takes the stage. They're called the Omega Fours, and they're pretty lousy. But that would just figure.

Turns out Mrs. P wouldn't allow Caitlin to spend the night again, so I walked her home. Maurice is waiting on the stoop when I return.

"You know, we could ride into the city together when we have to go to the theater."

"I have to go to Mr. Ross's house in the Village first. If I didn't get fired, that is."

"Oh, right."

"How's the play going?" I take a seat.

"Very difficult rehearsal today."

I think about Grand's mood. Maybe she was more upset about work than my missing walking Cleo at noon. "What happened?"

"Just one of those days when nothing works."

It has not dawned on me that *Arsenic and Old Lace* could flop. It did so well in the regionals, it's a shoo-in to be a hit. "Is your dad worried?"

"He's always worried." Maurice shrugs.

"I guess there's a certain amount of luck you need in the theater."

"Loads," Maurice says.

"So . . . are you looking forward to getting home to London?"

"I don't think about it," Maurice says.

"Caitlin will miss you."

"And I will miss her," Maurice says softly. "I'm going to turn in." He stands.

We say good night. Maurice goes into the apartment through the downstairs entrance. As soon as I hear the door snap shut and bolt, I call Andrew.

"How was the game?"

"We lost. I'm in the car with my family."

"So you can't talk?"

"Not really."

"Okay, check you tomorrow," I tell him.

This is one endless summer—and disappointing Grand makes it feel twice as long. After all she's done for me, I should be more responsible with my time. I swear I will never miss walking Cleo again. There's no groveling with Grand—I just have to earn her trust all over again (not easy).

I hang up and stretch my legs down the front steps. When I was in Indiana, all I did was dream of home. And now that I'm here, all I do is think about how great it was when I had my roommates to share everything with, whether it was schoolwork or social—no matter what was going on, they were there for me. I realize that I can't expect my friends to have missed me as much as I missed them, but I sure hoped that they would want to spend time with me again. Everything is different, and everything changed. I'm annoyed with myself that I didn't see it coming. The only thing that will save this crappy summer is a visit from my roomies. I have to make that happen. If I don't, I may lose my mind.

SIX

THE FINAL DAYS BEFORE THE FIRST PREVIEW OF A Broadway opening are always a tension convention. Grand gets nervous, and then day by day, before the actual opening night, she sheds her nerves and gets calm. "I rely on my technique as an actor," she says. "It never fails me. Experience plus technique delivers a professional result."

Today, though, Grand might as well be fifteen. She's having her final costume fitting. And now, the character comes to life in the mirror, and later, on the stage.

"Okay, Coral, give me a full three-sixty . . . nice and slow." The costume designer, Jess Goldstein, a trim, handsome professor type, watches as Grand turns in her costume, a vintage shirtwaist cotton dress in a floral pattern. Grand tightens the slim belt around her waist.

"I know I'm playing older," she says, "but I don't have to play frumpy."

"I think I'm going to add an apron," Jess says.

"I need a pocket for my notepad and pencil—she records everything her sister asks her to do," Grand explains.

The costume shop is a sewing room with several ironing boards, a washer and dryer, a sewing machine, and a work table. Grand is standing on a pedestal modeling her costume in front of a three-way mirror.

"Jess, what am I doing for shoes?"

"Vintage Hush Puppies." He smiles.

"Oh, thank you! I'll be so comfortable."

"Mary Pat is wearing the Cuban heel leather work shoe," Jess explains.

"Oh, I get the torture devices? Nice." Mary Pat Gleason bounds into the costume shop. She has curly brown hair and a quick stride. She is pretty but has what is called a "character face," which means she plays second leads and character roles. She has intense brown eyes that crinkle into half-moons when she smiles. And it seems like she's always laughing and smiling—at least when I'm around.

"I put gel soles in them," Jess tells her wearily.

"What's the matter? Can't take a joke?" Mary Pat

slips into the shoes. "Like butter."

Jess is visibly relieved. He ties a starched white eyelet apron trimmed in blue around Grand's waist. Grand looks at herself in the mirror. "I like it," she says.

Jess holds up his box of straight pins. "Okay, now I'm scared. You girls are way too agreeable."

"We're in a hit. Why complain?" Mary Pat says.

"Aren't you superstitious?" I ask. Even I, a mere runner in the lighting department, know you're never supposed to get cocky about success.

"Look, I've been doing this work since Hector was a pup. And I've been in some real turkeys—such messes I called them tetrazzini. But this one? We got it nailed. It's funny—and we're good. Right, Coral?"

"I'll let the *New York Times* decide."

"Oh, them." Mary Pat waves off the idea like a fat housefly. "You'll see. This baby will run."

Andrew assembles a series of opening shots for our Mermaid Day movie. He purses his lips tightly and stares at the screen. The only sound is the soft shuffle of clicks he makes on the images.

Mom and Dad have a small air conditioner in their office—not so much to keep them cool, but to keep the equipment cool. They are editing hundreds of hours of footage from their trip to Afghanistan. Renting the basement apartment to the Longfellows means that my dad didn't have to take a second job this summer—and he and Mom can focus on finishing their documentary instead of having to pick up jobs filming events like the fireworks on the East River on the Fourth of July, or driving to reservoirs upstate to film the drought levels in Albany.

A wipe-off board, covered with notes in Mom's handwriting, hangs over her desk.

Call Mary Murphy—news producer—has idea about sale

Dianne Festa has sell reel—call end of August

Disc 7—wobbly

Adam: Bob Barnett reps book tie-in author

Sometimes the things that Mom writes on the board stay up there for months. One of the first things I learned as a child, besides Never Wake Any Sleeping Family Member, was . . . *Do not erase the board. Not ever. Never.*

Dad has a metal stand filled with discs marked by day and locale, and organized by group. Sometimes their cameras recorded ordinary days, and sometimes they followed a group of news reporters into the worst zones of conflict in the war. My parents are so lucky that they weren't hurt. It makes me appreciate what they do even more. Someone is always filming the news on the television, and sometimes it's my parents. I appreciate how hard their job is—and I hope that the network uses their documentary as a news special. Mom thinks they have a potential buyer, and that's good news for us.

I have had a desk in my parents' work space since I was small. It started out kiddie size, and as I grew, so did the desk. Now I have one the size of my parents'; a farm table they found at a yard sale when we visited Dad's family in Vermont.

Maybe this is why I love to make movies and edit them: I have a place to work and the proper tools to execute my ideas. Mom and Dad always took my ideas seriously. Making movies and being with my parents were more fun to me than dolls, dressing up, or playing board games. My childhood play has now become my passion, or at least, that's how it seems. I'm sure it's the same for Andrew. We've always liked working in my parents' office, because everything we need to cut videos is here. And it's free. And no pesky Bozelli brothers bothering us. And then there's the lunch.

Mom brings a tray with thin-crust pepperoni pizza and Stewart's root beer (a bottle for each of us) and puts it on a work table. "How about a break?"

Andrew is syncing up the time codes on our Mermaid Day video. "Thanks, Mrs. C."

"How's it going?" Mom looks over Andrew's shoulder at the video monitor.

"We're getting there," he says.

"We're trying to find the story in the parade. It's coming off as just one flamboyant costume after another."

"That's what Mermaid Day *is*," Andrew says.

"We still need a story."

"Sometimes you can let the images speak for themselves. They don't need an over-veil. Just let the parade stand for what it is."

"See?" Andrew grins. "Your mom agrees with me."

"Don't gang up," I tell them as I click through to the steel drum band segment.

Andrew wheels his chair over to the work table. "Come on, I'm starving."

Mom sits down with us. "So, Viola, I got an email from Marisol's parents. You invited the girls for opening night? And you forgot to tell me?"

"I just floated the idea out there. I didn't think they could make it."

"Well, Marisol can. Her parents think it's a great idea for her to see New York for the first time with us."

"Do you mind?"

"Well, you know opening nights are always a big deal for Grand. And we'll be busy—but I think we can swing it. I want you to find out if Romy and Suzanne can make it. The sooner I know how many beds to prepare, the better."

Mom leaves the food and takes the tray and goes back downstairs.

"You have the coolest mom."

"I'm glad you'll be back from camp for opening night."

"Are you kidding? I wouldn't miss it."

Andrew and I roll our chairs back to the video monitors. He brings up the opening scene of the parade. I bring up my version, the scene with Olivia Olson across the boardwalk.

"Olivia is truly beautiful."

"She's all right."

Sometimes Andrew's lack of enthusiasm is annoying. I can't figure out why boys have to act like they don't like a girl when they are actually into her. It makes *no* sense. So I take him on. "No, Andrew. She *is* beautiful. And even when you break up with a person, you should take something good away from it, even if it's a surface thing—like an appreciation of her overwhelming and natural beauty."

"She's not my type."

"She's the only girlfriend you ever had. She is *totally* your type. You picked her. That *makes* her your type."

"I cannot be defined," he says as he clicks away on his type pad.

"Everyone can be defined."

"That just goes to show that you have no idea about me."

"What are you talking about? We've been best friends since kindergarten. I know everything about you."

"I don't know everything about you."

"Really."

"Really. You're a mystery to me." Andrew keeps his eyes on the Avid.

"What do you mean?"

"You're an enigma. One who cannot be understood. Let me give you an example. You flirted with Tag, and yet, you say you don't want him."

"I flirt for practice."

"Oh."

"I hadn't seen him in a year. And except for that email he sent to me at boarding school, I didn't think he knew I was alive. He's unattainable. Like Zac Efron. But that doesn't stop every girl on the planet from wishing they could date him."

"Tag noticed you. He made a point to talk to you. That means something."

This observation of Andrew's makes me smile.

"See? You know it," he says.

"There's nothing wrong with a little crush."

"I don't think so," Andrew agrees.

"I mean, as long as it doesn't get in the way of real life, who cares?"

"Right. Who cares? So Tag is your type?"

"I don't know. I guess. Maybe. That doesn't mean I'm *his* type."

"Oh, so you have to have a real shot with a guy in order for him to be your type."

"I guess so." I intercut Olivia across the boardwalk with a shot of a float that Andrew took. "Look at this."

"Nice," he says. Then Andrew looks at me. "Maybe . . . you're my type."

"Me? Are you kidding?"

He isn't kidding. But then he says, "Yeah. Gotcha."

"Whew." I fan my face dramatically. But what I really want to do is make Andrew feel absolutely fine at having said such a *crazy* thing and crossed such a wide line—the widest line in our friendship: the boy-girl barrier.

I think of Suzanne saying that Andrew liked me in

that way. Marisol kept telling me how cute he was, and Romy said something about "the path of least resistance" leading to love. But none of their observations added up, not until now, of course. Now I get it.

"I think we should cut the kettle drum band and go with the ukulele quartet," Andrew says.

This is, of course, what boys do when they are rejected, even if it's a fake rejection based on a joke. Boys get right back to business. But we are too close to just drop it. I don't want any weirdness between us. So I have to address the weirdness. "I think we should talk about your type."

"I don't think so."

"Maybe *I* want to talk about it," I tell him as I type a time code.

"I freaked you out," he says quietly.

"No, you didn't."

"I *totally* freaked you out." Andrew continues to look at the screen, leaning in as he edits a shot.

"If you did, I wouldn't be talking about it, I'd be avoiding it."

"Good point."

"I'm not going to let this affect our friendship, that's all."

"It wouldn't."

I learned a lot dating Jared Spencer, whereas Andrew learned next to *nothing* dating Olivia Olson.

I had a real exchange about filmmaking with Jared, whereas all Andrew did with Olivia Olson was run around to beauty parlors and orthodontists on a binge of self-improvement that rivals the transformation of Megan Fox.

Andrew has his head in the sand and in the video monitor when it comes to women. Romance affects *everything,* and it can kill a friendship. We need look no further than our own experience, by the way. Andrew doesn't hang out with Olivia anymore, and I don't email or Skype Jared. *It's over.* I don't ever want to lose Andrew Bozelli. *Ever.* No romance would be worth sacrificing our friendship. That would be the biggest mistake of my life. I count on him.

"Do me a favor," Andrew says.

"Sure."

"Let's forget I said anything."

I think for a moment. "Okay."

"I tell you whatever I'm thinking, and sometimes it's best not to," he says. "Besides, I didn't mean it. I was joking around."

A wave of relief rushes over me. "Okay." The wave of relief gives way to a bruised ego—just a little. "I guess."

Andrew keeps his eyes on the screen.

I won't let this awkward moment ruin our lifelong friendship. That's all this is. A blip. A smash cut in the middle of the action—not a fade to black.

I carry Cleo from Grand's kitchen to the living room. An envelope marked VIOLA is on the coffee table. I put Cleo down on the rug and sit.

I open the envelope.

Dear Viola,

You are doing a good job with Cleo. You've been on time every day. The extra money is to get yourself something nice for opening night. Love you, Grand

I take out six crisp twenty-dollar bills. A hundred and twenty bucks will buy me a fabulous vintage dress at Shady Lady's in the East Village. I can hardly wait to get over there and find something pretty. It pays to do a good job for Grand. She forgave me for my slipup, and I'll spend the rest of the summer proving I could be responsible.

I text Andrew from my seat, M101, in the Helen Hayes Theatre.

Me: At the theater. Waiting. You?

AB: Packing for camp.

Me: Don't forget the bug spray.

AB: I got a crate.

Me: Let's get the Mermaid video done before you go.

AB: Where are you later?

Me: I'll call.

My internship with Julius Ross, the world-renowned lighting designer, could be done by Cleo—it's basically drop off and fetch at its most difficult. Of course, I worked twice as hard after the coffee incident. I stayed after hours and volunteered for *extra* grunt work on top of my job, which can be described as grunt work. I fetch blueprints from his townhouse and bring them to his office on West 42nd Street, I pick up theater tickets to other shows and deliver them to whomever he has invited, and I even went to Hoboken, New Jersey, to sit in the work van while his assistant picked up some special lighting equipment. I'm basically a runner, and a professional bookmark. I hold the space while someone else gets the job done.

Grand says that I'll learn about lighting once the tech rehearsal is underway. That's when the lights are focused with the actors onstage and cues are set. The sound design is also implemented during this time, so all that wah-wah music Mr. Longfellow has played all summer will, at long last, have a purpose.

Today, there is nothing glamorous about the Helen Hayes Theatre. It's a factory. Without an audience, it's a black cave filled with rows of empty seats lit by bright, bare bulbs that dangle from the ceiling. This is the first day of load-in, where the sets for the play are brought from the warehouse where they were built. The work doors on the upstage wall are opened wide for the load-in. Daylight pours into the darkness. The sounds from the street are muffled, but the occasional siren cuts through, reminding everyone that the theater is not a sanctuary.

A semitruck is parked outside, filled with walls, joints, cornices, and steps that, once assembled and mounted, will become the set for the play. The components have been wrapped in fabric batting, marked for placement onstage like giant puzzle pieces. The large flats will become the actual walls of the living room of the Brewster home in *Arsenic and Old Lace*.

The theater has the same scent as the space in Phyllis Hobson Jones Hall at Prefect: paint, wax, and the last notes of old perfume, as though the matinee audience left in a hurry.

The air-conditioning is on, but the hot air from

outside blows through and creates a gust, causing me to shiver. The stagehands work in an organized fashion, as though they have done this a million times before. Occasionally they shout directions to one another or joke, but they never stop moving.

The crew head, Timmy Donovan, a man with muscles wearing an AAOL baseball cap, directs the guys as they carry the delicate stuff: strips of painted crown molding, windows, and stained-glass transoms of the era. Four men carry a set of assembled stairs, hollow on the inside, reinforced with cross braces, downstage left, where they place them carefully on the floor.

Through breaks in the batting, I can see that the walls are covered in vintage wallpaper, similar to a scroll of vines that I remember from my piano teacher's apartment in Brooklyn. Robin Wagner, a world-class set designer (George says), captured the authentic details of homes of the 1940s, right down to the doorknobs.

The production team, the designers and their assistants, confer with one another and occasionally look up and watch the proceedings from the house seats. They've created a temporary office with a makeshift folding table, propped over two rows of seats in the center of the orchestra. The table is littered with coffee cups from the Greek diner.

Neil Mazella, the set builder, has his long hair pulled back in a ponytail (he would have survived about ten seconds at the Grabeel Sharpe Academy with that hairstyle). He types into his laptop, lit by a makeshift work lamp with a bright bulb. He looks up and issues orders from his perch.

"Timmy, hoist the scrim."

A large black velvet drape attached to a long pipe hanging by hooks like those on a shower curtain is elevated by the stagehands from the upstage floor on pulley weights until it is suspended high and out of sight against the back wall.

"Looks good," Neil says.

If I squint, the load-in of a Broadway set is a lot like the Egyptians building the pyramids. There's a lot of hauling, lifting, placing, and levels to the action. I am watching the living room of a home being built from scratch; it really is like magic, which is the purpose of theater: to instill wonder and awe while gripping the audience with a good story.

Caitlin and Maurice join me in the aisle.

"Here's a surprise. How's rehearsal going?" I ask Maurice.

"It looks great. Dad is on edge, but he's always nervous at this point in the production."

"How's Grand doing?"

"She's hilarious. Brilliant," he says.

"No Dr. Balu today?" I ask Caitlin.

"I'm playing hooky," Caitlin says. "I hope you'll cover for me."

"No worries." But I am worried.

"I have to give this note to Mr. Mazella," Maurice says as he goes. Caitlin watches him go down the aisle to the work table, and I swear, the look on her face is *sad*. Maurice walks ten feet into the distance and she already misses him. Love is like the flu.

"I can't believe Maurice is going back to England when the play opens."

"I'm sorry."

"I finally find someone who I can't live without and I have to live without him." She sighs.

"Viola, take these schedules and place them in the dressing rooms," says the production runner. "I've got to get back to the studio."

"No problem." I turn to Caitlin. "Come on, I'll show you backstage."

Caitlin follows me down a side aisle and backstage. Charlie, the attendant, sits by the exit door on a stool working a crossword puzzle. "Barry told me to paper the dressing rooms," I tell him. Charlie doesn't look up.

"Uh-huh," he says, looking at his crossword puzzle.

Caitlin follows me through the wings to the stairs that lead to the dressing rooms. The actors' names are already on the doors. George has his own dressing room with a tiny attached bathroom because he's the lead. I leave a schedule on his makeup table.

We climb the steps to the second floor. Grand shares a dressing room with Mary Pat Gleason. I leave them each a schedule on their makeup tables.

"This is so cool," Caitlin marvels. "There's a whole life happening backstage. Not like an orchestra. We basically show up with our instruments, take our seats, and warm up. Actors have a home."

"Hopefully this one won't be temporary. Grand and George are praying for a long run."

Caitlin helps me paper the rest of the dressing rooms with schedules. The Brewsters, Mr. Witherspoon, Dr. Einstein, and the rest of the cast of *Arsenic and Old Lace* are about to move in. Opening night is becoming very real very fast.

"Hey, Viola," Barry hollers from the bottom of the steps. I go to the landing. "Good, you're sticking around. I need you to take a set of keys to Julius. He's at the production office on West Forty-second Street."

"Sure." I turn to Caitlin. "You want to come?"

"Okay."

Caitlin and I head out of the theater. "He can be a big grouch," I warn her.

We get into the elevator at 1511 Broadway and get off on the fourteenth floor. I hear Julius's big laugh coming from the conference room. I have learned not to linger and wait around outside when he wants something. I just get the guts and go right into a meeting and leave the envelope next to him. I tell Caitlin to wait outside for me, not that it would matter. He never looks up at me or says thank you.

The conference room table is filled with the designers and crew heads for the play. I leave the envelope next to Julius and turn to leave.

"Violetta?" Julius says. The room goes quiet. I turn.

"Do you mean me?"

"I don't see another Violetta around here."

"I'm Viola."

The designers and crew heads erupt in laughter.

"Julius gives his crew nicknames," Jess Goldstein says. Clearly, he can see that I'm mortified at having been singled out.

When I reach the door, Julius says, "Thanks, Viola."

"You're welcome," I say as I go out the door. The meeting resumes once I'm in the hallway.

"What happened in there?" Caitlin asks.

"I think I just became part of the team." As I press the elevator button, I smile. After my running all over the city and northern New Jersey, Julius Ross actually knows I'm alive. Now I know what Grand means when she says the theater is one big family. I think I just officially joined it.

The phone rings. I'll let the machine get it. Or Mom.

"Viola?" Mom calls up. "The phone is for you."

"Thanks!"

"You know, *you* can pick up the phone when it rings too."

"Sorry!" I shout.

"Hello?"

"Viola, this is Mrs. Pullapilly."

"Oh, hi, Mrs. P."

"Is Caitlin there?"

"I'm expecting her any minute," I lie. "She stopped to pick up some sunscreen for me at CVS."

"Do you mind telling her I need her home by three o'clock? I have an appointment and her father is expecting a delivery, and we need her home to sign for it."

"Home by three. No problem."

"Thank you."

I hang up the phone and grab my BlackBerry to text Maurice.

Me: Caitlin has to be home by three. Her mom just called me!
ML: Will do.
Me: She thinks Caitlin is with me. Tell her that I told her mom that she picked sunscreen up for me at CVS.
ML: OK.
Me: You guys should come over here. Cover my lie.
ML: We're in Central Park.
Me: Get on the train. Now.
ML: OK.

I know it will break Caitlin's heart, but I can't wait for Maurice to go home to the UK. Enough of this *Summer of the Sneak*. I've had it. I do not like being the peanut butter in the Caitlin/Maurice sandwich. I'm holding their entire romance together with excuses, providing a place to meet and a sympathetic ear for both of them.

If Mrs. P knew anything about acting, she would know I just gave a killer performance on the phone. But thank goodness she works in finance and can't read anybody's signals. Otherwise, we'd all be in big trouble.

SEVEN

SUZANNE HAS ARRANGED ANOTHER FOUR-WAY SKYPE from her mom's office. I log in.

"Hey, guys."

"Where were you?" Marisol asks.

"Mrs. Pullapilly called, and I had to cover for Caitlin."

"Still?" Romy shakes her head.

"I'm totally tense and freaked," I admit. "Sorry. Anybody have good news?"

"I do," Romy announces. "I can come to visit! My aunt is coming down to the city on business and can bring me with."

"And I'm taking Amtrak in and Romy's aunt is going to pick me up at Penn Station!" Marisol says.

"Fabulous! Suzanne, we wish you could make it. But

we totally understand," I reassure her.

"Don't write me off yet." Suzanne grins. "I'm coming—with my parents."

"What?"

"Yep, my dad is feeling a lot better, and he wants to come too. Mom is going to email your mom. We're going to drive in."

"I'll get the orange cone out *now* and reserve your space."

"You'd better. We want to see everything. Dad especially."

I think back to the Santry family when I visited them for Thanksgiving. They made me feel so at home. We saw so much of Chicago: the museum, Lake Michigan, and Grant Park. As hard as it was to be away from my own family for an entire school year, they stepped in and made the holiday fun. Now I get to return the favor. I'm going to make a list (points of interest, shops, restaurants, and parks) and a map (Brooklyn, Manhattan, the Bronx) of everything I want to show them: my New York City, the Viola Tour.

A full moon, pink and perfectly round like a Necco wafer, throws light onto our roof. Andrew and I have just polished off cold sesame noodles and are looking up at the sky over Brooklyn. We angled our chaise lounges for maximum planetary viewing.

"Where are Maurice and Caitlin?" Andrew asks.

"I have the night off from covering for them. Maurice is in the city having dinner with his dad, and Caitlin is home. She has family visiting. And I can't tell you how relieved I am."

"Look at it this way. When you get nervous, remember you are on the side of true love."

"I feel like those guys who walk a tightrope between skyscrapers. One false move and *bam*."

"What's the worst that could happen?"

"The *very* worst could happen. The Pullapillys could find out that we've been lying all summer, and that they can no longer trust us—and just as we enter tenth grade, they ban Caitlin from hanging with us. We could lose Caitlin forever. Her mother would love an excuse to send her to a convent school in India. Believe me, she *would* if she ever found out about Maurice."

Andrew leans back and looks up at the moon. "I don't want to go to camp."

"You'll make friends. You'll have fun. You'll lose a quart of blood a day to mosquitoes."

Andrew laughs. "I wish you were kidding."

"Why does Stewart's make the best root beer?" I

ask, holding it up to the light.

"It comes in a glass bottle. Plastic containers kill flavor."

"Do you know everything?"

Andrew blushes. "Not even close."

"What did you sign up for at camp?"

"Theater tech."

"That'll be fun."

"I went through the list of stuff to do that they offer, and one thing was more lame than the next. I don't want to learn how to make lye soap, nor do I like woodworking."

"Hope the food is good."

"It won't be. It's a *camp*. I'll be eating wilted lettuce and shepherd's pie. That is, if I'm lucky."

"Look at it this way. When they cook out, it will be better than Dad's," I remind him.

"No stretch there. What are you going to do while I'm gone?"

"Well, I have my internship. I'm told I'll really learn something about theatrical lighting during tech week at the play. Barry says he'll make sure I'm a part of everything. At this point, all I really know about lighting is that Julius Ross has a lot of crap that needs to be delivered."

"That's what an intern does, Viola."

"Right. I don't mean to complain. At least I'm observing the master," I agree with a sigh.

"Pretty soon it will be the end of summer. And then your roommates are coming. Your mom is turning this place into a hotel."

"I'm surprised she's not putting an air mattress on the roof. Every room has a couple of beds in it. My friends can't wait to meet you."

"Really." Andrew shifts his long legs and props them on the fence.

"They think you're cute." I decide it's okay to tease him, just a little.

Andrew laughs. "How do they know? Oh, right, when we Skyped."

"I told them you look better in real life."

"I look bad on Skype?"

"No, not terrible. A little pasty."

"Oh man. Pasty? That's gross."

"Well, maybe pasty isn't the right word. You look blue . . . ish."

"That's even worse. You're saying I have the skin tone of the underbelly of a lizard."

"It's not *that* bad," I say with a laugh. I'm glad Andrew and I are back to normal after the other day.

"I'll get a tan at camp."

"Good idea."

"So, I *do* look pasty."

"You are awfully sensitive." I swig my root beer.

"I guess I better go. The bus comes at six in the morning." Andrew gets up to go downstairs.

"How awful."

"You're telling me."

I place my bottle of root beer on the table to get ready to walk him out. I plan to come back up and call Marisol after I walk Andrew out. It's her night off from Target, and we get a lot of gabbing in.

Andrew turns and looks up. "That's a really bright moon."

"It's as big as the sun," I say, following his gaze.

"It just seems that way because it's close to the earth."

"The sun?"

"No, Vi, the *moon*."

"Why does it seem closer over Brooklyn than anywhere else?"

"I don't know."

"The moon seemed so far away in Indiana. But there, you could see the stars. Here, you hardly ever can."

"The city lights are too bright. They cancel out the stars," Andrew says.

"Call me from camp." I give Andrew a pat on the back.

"Are you serious? Of course I'll call. I'll be in the woods with nothing to do."

"What if there's no signal?"

We look at each other. "Oh no!"

Andrew puts his arms around me and gives me a hug. And then, just as I'm letting go of him, he pulls me close and kisses me.

Seriously. It is *happening.* Andrew Bozelli and Viola Chesterton are kissing on the roof of 345 72nd Street. I'm outside of my body watching this scene like the Channel 4 news team in a hovering helicopter. I can't believe it.

The kiss leads to . . . confusion.

I'm confused, because after all, I've only ever kissed Jared Spencer, and this kiss, of course, is completely different because it's delivered by a boy I have known all my life—before he had straight teeth and an excellent haircut. It's so weird to kiss Andrew, because I *know* him.

When I kissed Jared for the first time, it was like discovering the shore of a foreign country from the boat. I wasn't quite sure what I would find when I landed.

The gears in my mind race, and I almost hear a voice in my head say, "What does this mean? What does this mean? What does this mean?" But the rhythmic sound isn't the whirl of gears of repetitive thought in my head. The Melfis' exhaust fan from their air-conditioning chute on the next roof has kicked on in the heat.

"Bye, Viola," Andrew says, pulling away abruptly. He goes out the porthole and down the ladder. I can't move.

I just stay on the roof.

In the dark.

Just me and the giant pink moon.

What a relief, I'm thinking, as I pull open the work door to enter the Helen Hayes Theatre. I think I might major in theater when I get to college, because there's something about working in a cavernous and dark place that makes me feel as though anything is possible, and also, that it's easy to hide in this big, raw nothingness where plays are born.

I check my BlackBerry.

AB: I don't know what came over me last night.

Me: Me neither.

AB: Drop it?

Me: Dropped!

Andrew, my BFFAA (Best Friend Forever and Always), has now officially become my BFFAAAOKO

(BFFAA . . . And Only Kissed Once). I exhale a sigh of total and genuine *relief*.

I wish The Kiss had never happened. But it *did*. It's so much better to be friends. Once a boy becomes a boyfriend, you can't talk to him about what you're feeling, because he assumes whatever you're feeling is about *him* even when it's not. This was the takeaway from my year of dating Jared Spencer. And I would never want to trade my friendship with Andrew for a rooftop kiss. And once again, I'm going to have to deal with a surprising turn in my life story that I didn't see coming. (I count attending a year of boarding school as one of the most shocking turns my life has taken, but I survived it, and even ended up better for it.) Just goes to show you, sometimes you have to live in the moment and not worry about the big picture—as long as what happens in the moment doesn't *ruin* your life.

I turn my attention back to the task at hand. I'll focus on the play and let the Andrew thing vanish into thin air like a stage kiss. It happened, but it doesn't mean it's real life. Mr. Longfellow is onstage by himself, walking around. He doesn't look worried, he seems in control and ready for anything.

I've learned a lot hanging around this production. Of all the designers, and that would include Julius Ross,

Jess Goldstein is the nicest and actually says things about theatrical production that really stick with me. Jess taught me about mounting a revival versus a brand-new play. He likes the historical aspect of researching what the designers invented for past productions and reinventing them for a new audience. Also, when Les Longfellow wants something, Jess delivers.

I spent a day with the costume crew as they distressed the fabric for the dresses that the spinster aunts (Grand and Mary Pat) wear in the play. When Les Longfellow saw the costumes under the light, he felt they looked too new. Also, these are characters of modest means, who have one dress for everyday and one for church, and the one for everyday has been hand washed and pressed and worn for *ages*, so it should not look new.

Jess chose a deep forest green wool for Mortimer Brewster's suit. Brings out the hazel in George Dvorsky's eyes—he's the leading man and has to look scrumptious. Jess had the team tailor the suit just so, so George is truly the romantic lead down to the creases in his 1941 pants.

"Take a look at this hat." Jess comes out onstage with George, who is wearing the new suit.

Mr. Longfellow looks at the hat. "I don't like it."

"Laura?" Jess calls. Laura, one of his assistants, comes

onstage with another hat.

"This one is too Sinatra," Mr. Longfellow says.

"How about this one?" Jess takes the Sinatra hat off and places a second hat, this one with a wider brim, on George's head.

"I like it," Les says.

"I'll change the band. It should be deep gray—not black," Jess says.

"Fine," Mr. Longfellow says.

I'm amazed that something as small as a hat matters. But I've learned that everything matters when it comes to a play production; it's all about perfect details. I won't forget that when I'm cutting film.

The set is magnificent, a version of the original Broadway design, but beautifully rendered anew by the Great Robin Wagner. (Well, that's what Grand calls him. The Great is, like, his first name.) I may ask him to sign a poster for me.

Julius Ross, my boss, enters the theater, barking orders on his cell phone.

He is followed by what look to be three college-age assistants to the assistant. They blow past me and take over the entire work table. One assistant unrolls blueprints, while another opens a laptop. The head of the lighting crew emerges, a tall, burly man.

The stage manager gathers the actors onstage. Grand doesn't stand with George; she sticks with James Hampton, the famous character actor, with thick gray hair and a wide, warm smile, who plays the Rev. Dr. Harper, and Mary Pat Gleason, her character's sister, who has brown curly hair and drinks slowly from a water bottle without taking her eyes off the stage manager. She and Grand will be wigged for their parts, as neither of them appear as old in life as they need to in the play. The cast listens raptly as the stage manager runs through the schedule for the day.

"You can sit over there," Cameron, the head follow-spot operator, says to me.

We are high in the mezzanine, on a platform behind the audience. Three follow spots are rigged on stationary platforms. The two other operators, two guys in their twenties, stand at the ready and look to Cameron to tell them what to do. The lighting instruments are shaped like black metal rockets with a guide bar across the back to focus on the actor onstage. Inside these instruments is a wide, bright, single beam of light.

I slip the lens cap off my camera and flip it on. Using the light from the follow spots, I drink in the theater: the molding around the doors, the seats that are lined up like red dominoes, and then the stage.

From my point of view, the set is enchanting. I get a different sense of the color palette Mr. Wagner used from here. It looks like a mixing bowl from a country kitchen.

Pretty. Sturdy. And you want to hold it.

It's important in *Arsenic and Old Lace* to feel safe when you're watching it. After all, it's about two old ladies killing off unsuspecting men with a poisonous cocktail. They have a nutty brother who buries the bodies in the basement. The romantic element is about a man (George playing Mortimer) who isn't sure he wants to get married. It's a farce, so the set has the feeling of a pop-up book, with lots of doors, windows, and trapdoors so the characters can enter and exit, missing one another by a second or two, keeping the audience on the edge of their seats.

I zoom in and focus on the bench where the aunts keep the bodies. I'm going to film the backstage area (I've already gotten wonderful footage of the actors coming to work through the stage door). I plan to film the opening-night party, and then cut it together and give it to George and Grand as a keepsake.

Mr. Longfellow walks down the aisle to the lip of the stage. He is followed by his assistant and Maurice. I quickly flip the camera off. Mr. Longfellow looks up and surveys the light grid. The follow-spot operators stand at the ready like machine gunners on a ship while Mr. Longfellow confers with the stage manager.

Mr. Longfellow turns and goes back up the aisle to the last row of the theater to observe the tech.

The craft of operating the follow spot includes having to widen out the beam with one hand while guiding it with another. Mr. Longfellow likes to use follow spots to emphasize action in a scene, "to pointedly draw attention to it," which is why three instruments are engaged for a play that takes place on one set. Cameron wears a headset, taking instruction from Ravonne, who looks up at him from the orchestra and then back at the stage.

Grand stands downstage as the lights are focused on her. The light around Grand closes in tight around her, like a ray of afternoon light. From up here, a silky black shadow trails upstage until it diffuses to black. This is the moment in the play when Grand's character is scheming to serve a brew to the unsuspecting men that will kill them. The effect of the light conjures the meaning of the text. I lean forward and watch.

Grand stands patiently for a long time as Mr. Longfellow and Julius confer about the lighting.

After a while, George exits the stage. He returns moments later with a crate. Without saying anything, he places it behind Grand and invites her to sit. She looks up at George gratefully. George returns to his place as the director and lighting designer continue their heated discussion.

George Dvorsky is a true gentleman, and most of all, he anticipates what Grand might need, and tries always to put her first and make her comfortable—no matter what the situation. This is the definition of a perfect boyfriend—or *friend* period. Andrew is my George, but friend only.

Out of all of Grand's ex-husbands and former boyfriends, I like George the best. And not just because he is a great actor and he's tall and the closest thing I've seen to a chiseled Cary Grant type since, I don't know, Cary Grant himself. He's a good guy. And sometimes, more than anything I seek in a date—including brains, general hotness, athletic ability, or similar interests—*kindness* is the most important character trait of all. It means you will be treated with respect, no matter what. And as my mom is quick to point out, *respect* is the backbone of love.

EIGHT

THE R TRAIN NEVER HAS A CAR WITH AIR-CONDITIONING that works in the summer. Every single train car is hot; it's like riding in a Crock-Pot set on *stew*.

Maurice, Caitlin, and I are returning from Manhattan in a near-empty car that has the scent of chili fries and motor oil. When we reach the Bay Ridge Avenue stop, I stand. "Let's go, guys."

"We'll catch up with you later," Maurice says.

"But you're having dinner at my house. . . ."

Maurice and Caitlin shake their heads; they are *not* having dinner at my house as planned.

"You're *not* having dinner at my house?" I sit down as the doors close, missing our stop. But I don't care, I can double back at the next stop. "What's going on?"

"We only have five days left until opening night," Caitlin says.

"Yeah. So?"

"Once the play opens, Maurice goes back to England. We figured out that we have only a little more than seven thousand minutes left. And we want to spend as many of those minutes together as possible," Caitlin explains.

For a moment, I want to give Caitlin a lesson in *get real*, but she'll get enough of that if her mother ever finds out that she's been spending the summer riding trains into Manhattan to meet her boyfriend. The expression on Caitlin's face is pleading for me to understand.

"Please, Viola."

I take a deep breath. "Okay."

Maurice smiles at me. "Thank you."

"It was obvious to me that you were nuts about each other from the first moment you laid eyes on each other . . ."

Caitlin and Maurice nod that it's true, as they hold hands tightly, as if to hang on to each other, knowing this is not a dream.

". . . and long-distance *anything* is the worst. I get that. I just hope that everything works out for you. In the meantime, I have your backs."

The train pulls into the 77th Street station. I get off

on the ramp and turn to look back at the train, which pulls slowly out of the station. Maurice and Caitlin have their heads together, talking, as if one summer is not possibly long enough to fit in everything they have to say to each other. That must be what it's like when you find:

your forevermore love,

your true blue,

your one and only,

the person who totally gets *it,* in every possible way, every single day.

I'm happy for Caitlin and Maurice, even though my nerves are shot from worry. I just hope that seven thousand minutes will be filled with enough memories to last for both of them, once Maurice goes home for good.

"Don't you have to walk Cleo?" Mom asks from the doorway of my room.

"Grand doesn't have to be at the theater until three. So I have the morning off." I roll over in my bed and smash my face into the pillow. I forgot how much I love *not* having to show up for a job or an internship. I don't have to be at the theater until five. I do have a twinge of guilt; after all, I could be spending my downtime cutting all the footage I've taken at the theater. The more I do now, the easier it will be to cut the opening-night party later. I throw the sheet off me with my leg to get up.

Mom sits down on the edge of my bed. "We have a problem."

I sit bolt upright. "What happened?"

"Mrs. Pullapilly called and asked if Caitlin was here last night."

I jump out of the bed and yank my phone out of the charger to check it. There are no messages from Maurice. "What did you tell her, Mom?"

"I told her I had a meeting in Manhattan and that I was sure Caitlin was over, because she's always over. That seemed to make Mrs. Pullapilly feel better. Evidently, Caitlin missed her curfew. She was over an hour late."

My heart sinks in my chest. "Mom, Caitlin was supposed to be with me last night. But she wasn't. She was with Maurice."

"I see." Mom smooths the comforter on my bed. Then she stands and begins to make the bed. I get up and fluff the pillow. "So, Caitlin decided not to tell her mother she has a boyfriend?"

"She can't! You know how strict Mrs. Pullapilly is. Caitlin's life is on orange high alert every day. Don't you remember? We practically had to walk through a metal detector to go to Caitlin's thirteenth birthday party."

"They can be a little strict."

"A *little*? How about prison wardens in solitary confinement are more lenient!"

"You understand it's wrong for Caitlin to lie to her parents."

"Or for me to lie to you. I know. I totally get it. But I had a higher goal in mind. To honor and support the path of true love!"

My mother, who had a very stern look on her face (complete with the check mark worry lines between her eyes that she refuses on principle to Botox), smiles. "So the lie was noble?"

"Sort of. I'm dealing with a traditional value system here—ancient Indian—they are totally rigid, Mom. There's zero wiggle room. The answer to everything is *no*."

"Do you want me to talk to Mrs. Pullapilly?"

"No way. She'll make it worse for Caitlin. And it's all my fault. They fell in love on our roof. It's like we set the stage for the drama."

"I don't think Mrs. Pullapilly would hold you responsible just because they happened to meet at our house."

"Mom, are you kidding? The Indian people are mystical. They find meaning in *everything*. A locked door is a symbol, a ray of light is a spiritual indicator. I could go on and on. There are no accidents! Caitlin says that *all* the time. Her aunt Naira is, like, an expert about the world beyond."

"Maybe Aunt Naira could talk to Mrs. Pullapilly."

"She's in India." I sit down on my bed. "Sometimes I wish Maurice had never come here at all."

"Let's talk this through," Mom says. "How serious are they?"

"Enough for Caitlin to risk any of the freedom she has to see him."

"I see."

The look on my mom's face says, *Time for the tough questions. And the honest answers.* But the truth is, my parents have been honest with me about everything—okay, maybe not finances, but everything else about life, work, and love is on the table, and always has been.

My teacher in middle school actually let me lead the health class discussion about reproduction, because my mother taught me the mechanics in a very matter-of-fact way, much the same way my father taught me how to use a camera. I think Mom might be concerned that Maurice and Caitlin are getting way too serious way too fast. I'm not worried about my friend and her new boyfriend; I'm worried about her parents.

"When she comes over here to visit me, it's not to

hang out with me, but to go someplace with Maurice."

"Where do they go?" Mom asks.

"They come to the theater to watch rehearsal. Or they go to the movies. Or they walk on the Promenade. Maurice took her into Manhattan to Eighth Street. They went to Lafayette Bakery for cupcakes. Last night they were on the train coming back to Brooklyn with me and they didn't get off at our stop. They just kept going. They have only seven thousand minutes left to be together before Maurice goes back to London. I mean, that alone—the fact that they did the math on the exact amount of minutes they have left this summer—should tell you how devoted they are to each other."

"You should encourage Caitlin to tell her mother about Maurice."

"Mom, you don't get it. She's not allowed to date *anyone*. And it's worse—even if, let's say they allowed Caitlin to date, they'd never let her date a British guy. At least you and Dad would let me go out in a group. Caitlin can sort of do that, but believe me, Mrs. P doesn't think our group includes a boy who likes Caitlin *that* way."

Suddenly the summer, which has seemed so long because I have been asked to keep a secret, isn't. I want to tell my mom everything. So I keep going.

"The Pullapillys have a plan for her. A life plan! After

high school, and she'd better be valedictorian because they want her to go to Juilliard and become the greatest violinist who ever lived, they plan to pack up and go back to India, and choose a husband for her. Then they'll all live in the same house, forever. That's right. *Everybody.* Caitlin and her handpicked husband and their eventual children and her parents."

"My goodness." My mom never says things like *My goodness*. She is really thrown for a loop right about now. "Viola, what do you think she ought to do?"

"I don't know, Mom."

"What would you do?"

"Mom, can I tell you something?"

"Anything."

"You know I had a boyfriend at Prefect."

"The filmmaker."

"Jared."

"You haven't told me very much about him."

"Because he turned out to be a dork."

My mom laughs. "That happens."

"Well, even though he was a dork, he actually ended up being the perfect first boyfriend. We talked a lot on the phone and emailed, and then when we could, we'd go somewhere with a group. Like a concert—or once, a one-woman show. I never felt like I was thrown into it.

It built in little steps. It didn't rule my life."

"That's good." Mom smiles.

"But for some girls, boys rule their lives."

"Why do you think that's true?"

"They finally feel special when they have a boyfriend. And in Caitlin's case, she feels *free*. At long last, she has her own life outside of her family. I think that's part of the reason she fell so hard for Maurice."

"And what about Maurice?"

"I think Maurice was fated to be with an Indian girl. He loves the culture. He likes the country, the food, and the art. Plus, growing up in London, he knows a lot of Indians. And I think he took one look at Caitlin, and he saw fate."

"That can happen."

"It *did* happen, Mom. I saw it. What should I do?"

"You should tell Maurice and Caitlin that they were very lucky. You and I covered for them this time, and while you are happy for them, you are *not* happy with the way they are handling Mr. and Mrs. Pullapilly. You tell them that they cannot ask you or me to lie."

"Okay, Mom."

"We have a big week ahead of us. And we want Caitlin to be a part of it, right?"

"Absolutely."

"So tell them not to ruin the fun for everybody."

"Got it."

I don't want *anything* to ruin my roommates' first trip to New York City. And I want Caitlin with us every step of the way, not grounded and hidden away in her apartment, playing scales on her violin, pining for her final moments with Maurice. I have to get to them and set the ground rules before it's too late.

Me: How's camp?

***AB:** Stage manager for Sophie Treadwell's Machinal.*

Me: Sheesh.

***AB:** All girls in the cast. Loving it.*

Me: Sure you are. Your haircut is getting the snaps.

***AB:** What can I say? Met a great girl here. Mel.*

Me: Congratulations!

***AB:** Yeah. We hit it off right away. She actually makes this place bearable.*

Me: Great!

***AB:** I was dreading camp, and now I don't want to leave.*

Me: Wow.

***AB:** Mel's from California. Bummer. Talk to you later.*

Talk about snark. Andrew Bozelli got on a bus, went to Maine, put down his duffel, picked a bunk, and became a jerk. All-girl cast and a new girlfriend? Like the 6.1 Avid program I learned in 2008: I am obsolete.

I click on the video iChat on my Mac. Romy and Marisol are on-site already.

"Hey guys," I chime in.

"Mom says I have to bring a dress for opening night," Marisol says.

"You should. It's medium fancy."

"Can't I wear something comfortable?" Romy moans. "It's not like I'm gonna be onstage. The only dressy dress I have is a hand-me-down. Spaghetti strap thing from my stepsister Marina. She only wore it once, so it's like new. It's pretty. A lot of ruffles. Will that work?"

"Sounds gorgeous," Marisol says. Marisol is always supportive of personal expression through fashion.

"Wear whatever you want."

"What's the matter, Viola?" Marisol leans in.

"One kiss and my friend turned into a frog."

"Tag?" Romy asks.

Suzanne joins the iChat. "I knew it. Tag called!"

"No, he did not. This is about Andrew."

"Let me guess. Andrew likes you," Suzanne says triumphantly. "Like a girl."

"Not exactly. Before Andrew left for camp, he came over and hung out, and on his way out, he kissed me."

Romy sits back, while Marisol lets out a *woo-hoo*. Suzanne congratulates herself knowingly. "Continue."

"Yeah, well, before you spray paint our initials in a big lemon yellow heart on the South Bend overpass, listen to this. I've been kissed by a boy who *really* likes me, and then Andrew. And I think Andrew was just practicing."

"How insulting." Marisol is amazed.

"How do you know you were a practice round?" Romy asks.

"Because he has a slew of girls up at camp."

"Who would have thought it? Your BFFAA has become a *guy*. Well, it happens to the best of them."

"Thanks, Suzanne. Now I feel worse."

"Do you like him?" Marisol asks.

"I don't think it's too much to ask, when you're fifteen years old, that when it comes to friendship, the terms of the friendship do not change over time."

"You miss the old Andrew," Marisol says.

"I miss the *normal* Andrew. I don't need drama from Andrew Bozelli. I don't want to be uncomfortable around my best friend."

"Fair enough," Romy says. "Too bad there aren't referees in life like there are in field hockey."

"No kidding. Because Andrew went over the line. I should have stopped him before he kissed me, but the truth is, I didn't see it coming. I was caught up in the moment. And then there was this big pink moon, and there's just something about rooftops in Brooklyn . . . oh, I don't know. It got out of hand and crazy and all so fast."

"You *have* to talk to him about it," Marisol reasons.

"It's too awkward now. Totally weird. He's turned into a boy. He brags about all these girls at camp who are after him. I expect this kind of thing out of guys like Jared Spencer, but not Andrew."

"Well, let's not let Andrew and his weird self ruin our trip to New York City," Romy says practically. "This is a big deal that we're all coming. We need our time together, because when the fall comes, we are one girl short in our quad."

"I *know*," I groan.

"If Andrew wants to behave himself and be your BF and our BF once removed, then he's welcome. But if he can't hack it—then he's out. Agreed?" Suzanne says.

I take down Marisol's train information, Romy's aunt's cell number, and Suzanne's ETA in the car with her parents. We click out of the iChat, and as the screen goes to black, so does my mood.

The most difficult thing about Andrew and me is that I've lost him for good. If I had a problem with a boy, or a crush that went unrequited, when I needed to talk about it, it was Andrew I would turn to. I don't feel like I have my BFFAA to talk to anymore, and this is the great loss of the summer of 2010.

NINE

IT'S BEEN RAINING FOR DAYS. I HOPE IT CLEARS UP soon. I don't want anything to ruin the Prefect Academy Quad Reunion. I walked Cleo through the downpour, which, in the heat of August in New York City, is like walking a dog when it's raining consommé. When the raindrops hit the sidewalk, they actually *steam*.

Julius Ross had a billion errands for me to run during previews, which are the two weeks of performances that precede opening night. This is when the technicians and the actors get the final kinks out of the show, with a live audience. A few days before opening night, the critics come to review the play, and run what they've written on the morning after opening night.

Grand and George, so used to performing the play

from the long run in Ohio before it moved to Broadway, have jitters, but they aren't as bad as they would be if they hadn't had the regional run. They are pretty calm for a couple of actors in an important revival about to be reviewed by every newspaper, magazine, and blog.

It's three hours until curtain for the critics' review, but I know where to find Grand. She makes it a habit to arrive at the theater early, to prepare slowly and make her face up methodically before the show. There are all kinds of actors, and Grand is the prepared type.

Backstage, the scent of hair spray from the wigs and starch from the costume room wafts through. It has the scent of the corner at the intersection of Fern and Maple in Bay Ridge, where the Wang Chinese Laundry is next door to the Lynne Watkins Beauty Shop. I take the stairs up to Grand's dressing room.

Grand sits with her face in her hands in front of her makeup mirror. The lightbulbs around the mirror are round and bright, like a row of suns. They're as bright as the light they use at the dermatologist's office. "Come in, hon," Grand says.

"Wow. Roses." A lush arrangement of flowers with a small glass charm of a bottle marked POISON sits on the makeup table.

The card says, *Knock 'em dead,* which is hilarious,

because Grand spends the play poisoning unsuspecting men.

"From Daryl Roth," Grand says. "Class act. And I can't say that too often about producers I have known."

"You okay?"

"Oh, your grand is just a little blue." She smiles, the opposite of blue.

"Why? You open in three days."

"I know. And I feel this is as solid a show as I've ever been in."

"So what's the problem?" I sit down in the chair next to Grand.

"I was thinking this might be the last time I'm in a show on Broadway, and I get a little wistful thinking about my life and my career, and the plays I've done. The roles I'll never do. There's less ahead for me than behind me, and you know, that's a . . . bummer."

"You're worried about death?" I can't believe it. It's strange for my grandmother, who immerses herself in life, to think about death, and worse, to let it bother her. But this is the actor's life; it's loaded with drama—or maybe just dramatic thoughts.

"No, no. Just thinking about when I won't be able to act anymore. And maybe this is it. The swan song, and you know, nobody told me. I just got lucky at this stage of my life, and this role came to me. I have lots of friends who aren't working, and a few who will never work again. And certainly not on Broadway."

"Grand, you've been saying this for years. You aren't upset about the passing of time, you're just dealing with all the actor stuff. Do you know a single actor who believes she gets the roles she *should* be getting?"

"Not one. We are grousers and complainers."

"But you have *no* reason to be *sad*. You're about to open on Broadway."

"I know. But it's been twelve long years since I've been on Broadway."

"And, it's not like you've been sitting around. You did a bunch of plays in regional theater. One after another. Really *good* parts. And what about that film role—you were a chef in *Julie and Julia*."

"Oh, that was nothing. A drive-by."

"You were good."

"Thank you, honey. Movies are nice, but there's nothing like the theater. Movies are like unrequited love; you play the part imagining you might reach someone, and when you play a part in the theater, you *know*. The audience tells you everything. You have a partner."

"So, okay, good. Chin up already. This is not the last stop in your career. Think about all those actresses that you admire who worked until they were much older than you."

"Who?"

"Helen Hayes and Claudette Colbert."

"Good point."

"And don't forget Lauren Bacall. She's still at it. Why not you? Don't limit yourself. You have many, many shows ahead of you. And someday, I want to direct you in a great play. So you can't quit until my dream comes true."

Grand looks into the mirror. Her blue eyes go steely and she squints. This is the look she gets when she's in the kitchen mastering a new recipe, or when she does Malibu Pilates. "Now, *that's* a goal. You and me. Together. Working on a play. The baton passed from grandmother to granddaughter. It's brilliant, and we haven't even chosen the play." Grand looks at me and smiles. "But we *will*."

Grand sponges makeup onto her face in small dabs, until the surface is as smooth as marble. She takes a small angled brush and, with tiny strokes, changes her blond eyebrows to white. She takes a palette of blue and one of gray and, swirling it, gives herself half-moon bags under each eye. I watch as her face ages with powder and paint, and she becomes Aunt Martha, half of the killer spinster sisters in *Arsenic and Old Lace*.

"You know what?"

Grand looks at me. "What?"

"You finally look like a real grandmother."

Grand looks in the mirror, and then looks at me. "And you've been waiting for that?"

"All my life."

And then, we do what we always do. We laugh and laugh.

I slip down the stairs from Grand's dressing room to backstage. Maurice and Caitlin stand inside the backstage door.

"You want to watch the show with me?" I ask.

"Sure," Caitlin says.

"I've got to run an errand for Dad." Maurice looks at his watch.

"We'll be in the light booth," I tell him.

It's been difficult to get any time alone with Caitlin, and we need to talk. As we enter the cold theater, I exhale a sigh of relief. Now I'll be able to tell her what I have been meaning to say all summer.

"Caitlin . . . ," I begin.

"I know what you're going to say."

"I don't think you do," I whisper as we climb up the

work stairs to the lighting booth.

"You're going to tell me to be careful, not to get caught with Maurice." I've never heard this tone of snark before coming from Caitlin, so I stop and look at her.

"No. I was going to say, you need to tell your parents about Maurice. He's leaving for England, anyway—so this is a good time to tell them you've met a nice boy and you like him."

"You can say those kinds of things to your parents, but I can't to mine. They would be disappointed in me."

"You won't know unless you tell them."

"I never will, so please don't ask me to." Caitlin's eyes fill with tears. "I need to keep this secret . . . and I'm asking you to do the same for me."

"Okay, okay," I tell her. I didn't mean to make Caitlin cry, but this is certainly a sign of exactly how important Maurice is to her. "I'm sorry."

"Thanks," Caitlin says as she sits down on a stool in the light booth. "It will all be over soon anyway."

Mom, Dad, and I take a flashlight and head down to the basement. The cold, clammy temperature and the scent of old wine barrels comes at us in a blast as we make our way down the stairs.

"I think it's over here, Adam," Mom says, pointing to

a corner with stacked wooden risers, which my parents use when they film a tracking shot. "Behind our stuff."

Dad directs the beam to the far wall. "There it is. Girls, give me a hand."

Dad places the flashlight on a box. He sorts through the junk, and then pulls a wooden ramp with notches that fit our brownstone steps out of the pile. "You know, when the Martinellis told us they were leaving this behind, I never thought we'd need it."

"See why I don't throw anything away?" Mom says knowingly. "You never know when you'll need something."

"Girls, take a side and help me get this up the stairs." Mom and I help him carry the homemade wooden wheelchair ramp up the rough-hewn steps.

We get the ramp into the kitchen. "Vi, go and get the flashlight," Dad says, wiping the sweat from his face onto his sleeve.

"This thing is heavy," Mom remarks.

I run back down to the basement and grab the flashlights, taking the stairs two at a time.

"Okay, heave and then ho," Dad says.

We guide the wheelchair ramp through the hallway to the front door. I push the doors open. Mom and Dad follow, carrying the ramp. Mom places the end of the ramp at the top of the stairs and Dad runs to the bottom and snaps it into place.

"It's not warped at all," Mom marvels.

"This is gonna work," Dad says.

I put my arms around my parents. "Thank you so much. This means the world to Suzanne and her mom."

"Hey. That's what friendship is all about," my dad says softly. He doesn't let go of my mom and me for a long time, just like when I was a kid, just like when I was small.

At long last, my roommates are arriving! Finally, they will see Brooklyn, meet Caitlin and Andrew, and of course, Maurice—and see their first actual Broadway show, starring my grandmother.

I wait on the steps of our house, with my camera ready to film the arrival of Romy and Marisol. Her aunt's car peels around Avenue J and onto our street. Romy hangs out the back window when she sees me.

I get a nice shot of the car as it sails through the cul-de-sac.

"Viola!" Romy hollers, and waves from the window.

"We made it!" Marisol says.

Romy's aunt pulls up in front of our house and double-parks. I run down the steps. Romy and Marisol get out of the car, looking so chic. Romy wears red-and-white-striped espadrille platforms, skinny jeans, and a field hockey jersey, while Marisol wears a flowery sundress and gold gladiator flats.

"Oh my God, this is so cool and exactly as you described it." Marisol looks around and marvels.

"Welcome to Brooklyn! You guys found each other at the train station—no problem, right?"

"So easy. Romy and Aunt Sally were waiting for me in Penn Station, just like we planned. I came off of the Amtrak train and there they were."

"This is my aunt Sally," Romy says.

I shake Aunt Sally's hand. She has a good athletic grip (must run in the family) and a short haircut.

"You'll be okay?" Sally says to Romy.

"Oh yeah." Romy gives her aunt a hug. "See ya."

"I'll pick you up in the city on Sunday."

"Great," Romy says.

Aunt Sally jumps into her car and backs out of the cul-de-sac. Romy, Marisol, and I can't believe we are back together; it seems like years. We throw our arms around one another.

"Come on. I'll show you where you're staying." I pick up Marisol's and Romy's backpacks, and they grab their duffels and follow me into the house.

"Ma, they're here!" I shout.

Mom comes out of her office and gives Marisol and Romy a hug on our way up to dump their stuff in my room.

"Here we are." There's hardly any floor space in my room. Mom and Dad put two air mattresses down and pulled out the trundle so my single became a quad, just like we had at Prefect. "Sorry it's so small."

"It's perfect," Marisol says.

"How cool. You can see the whole neighborhood from up here," Romy says, looking out the window. "Hey, it's Suzanne."

A horn honks as the station wagon pulls into place in front of our house. Suzanne gets out of the car. Her blond hair glistens from three stories up. Romy waves and shouts out the window.

"Come on, guys," I tell them as I start down the stairs.

"They're here!" I call out to my parents. "The Santrys!"

We race down the stairs and out onto the stoop. Mrs. Santry is in the back of the wagon, unloading Mr. Santry's wheelchair. My mom comes down the stairs, and Dad joins us from the backyard.

I turn on the camera and begin to film their arrival.

"Hi, Mrs. Santry," I call out. She looks up at me, and when she sees I'm filming her, she smiles and waves me off.

I walk down the steps, holding the camera steady.

I ask Mrs. Santry, "How was your trip?"

"It was great," she says.

I go around to the side of the car and put my head in the window. "Hey, Mr. Santry."

"Viola, I'm locked and loaded and ready for Broadway."

I go in for a close-up of Mr. Santry, who smiles. He is an older version of his handsome sons.

"You better be," I tell him. "We have orchestra seats."

"Fantastic."

Suzanne opens the car door for her father. "Dad was in *You Can't Take It with You* in high school."

"That is correct. I was a thespian." He laughs. "Not a good one, but I had a lot of enthusiasm."

I step back and film the introductions. My dad enters the shot.

"Bob, I'm Adam Chesterton."

"Good to meet you, Adam."

"Let me give you a hand," Dad says. Mom and Mrs. Santry chat as they unfold the wheelchair.

"Is this the best, or what?" Suzanne says. She puts her hands on her hips and smiles at us. I don't know why, and probably never will, but whenever Suzanne is around, I feel I can breathe a sigh of relief—it's as though everything is under control when she arrives. She is our leader, and we all look to her for wisdom *and* an agenda. "What should we do?"

I film her as she drags her duffel out of the back of the car.

"Come on, let's get your stuff upstairs," I tell Suzanne. Romy and Marisol grab the Santrys' suitcases. I flip the camera off and help Suzanne carry her duffel up the stairs.

"Mom and Dad set your parents up in the front parlor."

We stop while Suzanne takes in the parlor. Romy and Marisol drop the bags by the sofa. Mom put two roll-away beds in the center of the room and placed the sofa and chairs around it.

"Excellent." Suzanne points to the old-fashioned front windows, with a view of the green leaves of the elms. "Mom and Dad will love it."

Suzanne goes to the windows and looks out. Marisol, Romy, and I join her. We watch through the window as my dad helps push Mr. Santry in his wheelchair up the ramp we just dragged out from the basement. "The ramp is cool," Suzanne says.

"It came with the house," I tell them.

"How lucky is that?" Suzanne smiles. "Let's go!"

Suzanne, Marisol, and Romy follow me up the front

stairs. I show them Mom and Dad's office, and my desk. Then I take them up to my room. Marisol takes charge and shows Suzanne where the bathroom is, and where to put her stuff.

I watch Suzanne unpack, and just like we were at Prefect Academy, we fall into a rhythm. Marisol sits cross-legged on the trundle, while Romy stretches out on an air mattress. Suzanne goes into a long story about working at the Dairy Queen, and how it took her three weeks to master the dip cone, and the day she did she felt like she had split an atom and isolated a genome to save mankind. *That's* how hard it is to master a dip cone.

I stand in the doorway and listen and think how lucky I am to have ever met these girls. We move together like a pinwheel, each of the four foil prongs moving in one direction, picking up light.

And I think about Suzanne saying how lucky it was that we had a ramp in the house for her dad, when in fact, it's unlucky what happened to him—that he has MS and can't walk. But Suzanne *would* think the ramp was lucky, and that her parents driving her here was lucky, and that tickets to a Broadway show make her luckier still. She wouldn't for one minute be sad about what she *doesn't* have, because she's grateful for whatever she *does* have.

Just like Mom says, and she's said it more times than I can count: *It's all in how you look at things.*

The soft yellow centers of the Chinese lanterns dangling from a wire over the picnic table throw light on what is left of our feast. Dad made his red hamburgers and black hot dogs (same grill, same father, same technique, same results). But Mom made a delish Mexican casserole, fresh rolls, and a big salad, so Dad's grilling was set off by food we could actually eat.

"Come on, Bob. It's been a long day," Mrs. Santry says.

"Thanks, guys, this was delicious." Mr. Santry smiles at my dad and mom. "We appreciate your hospitality."

"Bob, it's great to have a guy around here. All I got is women."

"I wouldn't complain." Mr. Santry laughs.

Dad throws open the gate and pushes Mr. Santry up the walkway on the side of our house, to take him up the ramp and into the front parlor. Mrs. Santry follows them out. I'm surprised at how easy it is to adapt our house to Mr. Santry's wheelchair.

"I'm going to finish up in the kitchen," Mom says. "Thank you for doing the dishes."

"You're welcome," Marisol, Suzanne, and Romy say.

"Well, it's a festival of girls," Maurice says as he

opens the gate for Caitlin.

"Hi, everybody," Caitlin says.

My roommates greet Caitlin as though she is the fifth roommate. I've told them so much about her, and she knows everything about them, so there's no learning curve; it's just as if Caitlin has known the girls all her life.

"There's pineapple upside-down cake," I offer.

Caitlin's cell phone buzzes. "Excuse me," she says as she checks it. "Hi, Mom. I'm at Viola's. Yes, all her roommates are here. . . . Okay, I'm on my way."

"You have to go?" Marisol asks.

"Yep. Sorry."

"I'll walk you to the corner," Maurice says.

As soon as they're out of earshot, Romy says, "You weren't kidding. That isn't a cell phone—that's a tracking device."

"I had a talk with Caitlin."

"How did she take it?" Marisol asks.

"She won't tell her parents about Maurice. And besides, he's leaving after opening night."

"The director doesn't stay and watch the play for the run?"

"No. A theater director gets the play to opening night, and then they're on to the next job. The stage manager keeps the show fresh with the instructions of the director, and also handles the understudies, and the day-to-day of running the show."

"Do you think the play is going to be a hit?" Romy asks.

"I hope so. I mean, I like it, but I like old movies. And this is an old play."

"I'm back from the abyss," Andrew says from the kitchen door.

"Andrew!" I stand up at the table.

"And look, I survived." He sure did. Andrew has a tan. His haircut has grown out a bit. And I can't believe it, but he looks (even) taller. "The mosquitoes didn't kill me."

Andrew wears his best pale blue Ralph Lauren polo shirt and a pair of jeans. Gone are the days when he wore sweatpants and hand-me-down Gap T-shirts. Now that he's a ladies' man, he dresses like one.

I introduce Andrew to my roommates, and they shoot one another knowing looks. The Chinese lanterns may not throw a lot of light, but they can see everything clearly—at least where Andrew is concerned.

"So, tell us about camp." I cut Andrew a slice of cake.

"It was cool." He smiles.

"Viola said you were tech director for a play," Marisol says.

"Oh yeah. I was the only guy who knew how to rig

equipment. And I filmed the performance too."

"Can't wait to see it."

"It's not bad."

"How's Mel?" I ask.

"She went back to California."

"So, now you're totally free?" Romy says.

"Not really." He smiles.

"How can you keep it going? She lives in California," Marisol says.

I could crawl under the table. My roomies have turned into the Bennet sisters in *Pride and Prejudice*. They're grilling Andrew like he's a *suitor*, instead of my BFFAA from Planet Platonic.

"Long-distance enchantments never work," Suzanne says.

Andrew shrugs. "You girls manage to stay friends with each other—and you live in different states. It's a challenge, but it's worth it. Right?"

"How would you like to have an ocean between you?" Maurice pushes the gate open. "I won't see Caitlin for a very long time. Unless Dad gets a job in New York again."

"Maurice has it the worst," Romy says. Romy can relate to Maurice because of her yearlong crush on Kevin Santry.

"Well, let's not think about it. Caitlin is cleared to come on our tour of Manhattan, and her mom says she can come to opening night. So, you have a lot of good times ahead, Maurice." I try to boost his spirits.

"Thanks," he says softly.

"It's going to be fun. We'll make sure you have a good time. Maybe you won't get *everything* you want, but you'll get something wonderful," Marisol says.

"Walk on the bright side," I agree.

"I haven't a choice," Maurice says.

The Lasko fan throws warm air around my room. Suzanne is on one air mattress, Romy on another, while Marisol is in the trundle. I stretch out on my bed.

"Andrew is *way* cuter in real life than he is on Skype," Romy says.

"You think so?"

"Viola, he likes you. And I think Mel is a made-up person."

"No way. He never lies," I assure Suzanne.

"He didn't have too many details about her," Marisol concurs. "When a boy really likes a girl, he can describe her. He never even said what she looked like."

"For a guy with a camera, he had no pictures," Suzanne says.

"Andrew would be too shy to show pictures. He's very private. He never talks about girls to me."

"He seemed awfully anxious to tell you about Mel when he was at camp," Romy reasons.

"True. But remember, I had to *pull* things out of him about Olivia."

"Yeah, but how much did he like her—really? He's being cavalier. He knows you'll be in school with him this fall, so all of a sudden, he has to act like he's not interested in you despite what he's said and done this summer."

"What a waste of time," Marisol says.

"That's a boy for you," I agree.

"He's just insecure," Suzanne says. "He kissed you, Viola, but he isn't sure he should have—or that you wanted him to."

"It was so weird, I don't even know what to say about it. I think he was leaving for camp and was sad for a second. It's just one kiss. We agreed to drop it, and never talk about it."

"You don't like him like you liked Jared Spencer?" Marisol asks.

"I can't even compare the two. I've known Andrew all my life. And Jared was cute and I met him at a party. It's totally different."

"Nothing was at stake with Jared Spencer," Marisol says.

"*Nothing.* Remember how they herded us up on the bus and took us over with peppy Trish as our chaperone—for that dance? I mean, if you met someone and you never wanted to see him again, no problem—we got back on the bus and went back to Prefect. It's not like we had to see those guys every day—or at all. With Andrew, it's different. We go to school together, we make movies together—we hang out."

"You only like him as a friend?" Suzanne says.

"I need him as a friend. I don't know what I'd do if he wasn't my friend, and I don't know how to think of him any other way."

"Well, then you have to tell him that you're not interested in him in that way. Then you can get back to normal and being best friends. Otherwise, he'll keep hoping you'll change your mind. He'll keep torturing you with all these stories of made-up girlfriends and have to do his macho act to impress you."

"It's so annoying," I admit. "I liked it so much better when we talked about everything. Now it's awkward."

"If I wasn't in love with Kevin Santry, who I can never have, so forget it, I will never be your sister-in-law, but if I wasn't in love with Kevin, I would totally go for

Andrew," Romy says. "You know, in the spirit of friendship—to help you out."

"Riiight," I say.

We laugh. And just like at Prefect, back in our quad, we never ended conversations at night before sleep, we'd just sort of drift into silence. We'd exhaust a subject and begin another, but one by one, we'd fall out of the conversation entirely and go off to sleep.

The whirl of the fan is comfort. I lie awake and stare at the ceiling, and without a word being said, as my roommates, tired from long days of travel, go to sleep, I imagine that a few days from now, when they go, the loneliness will set in. I have figured out, through all the good-byes, whether it's my parents leaving on assignment, or Grand on tour, or my roommates returning home after a year at Prefect, that I'm not very good about saying good-bye. In fact, I worry about it long before I have to say the words and live through it. I have a hard time putting aside my feelings.

For a girl like me who was a loner, I like having my roommates around, even when we aren't doing anything in particular. A room full of friends became a big plus to me as an only child. It's just nice to see someone studying across the room, or knowing you have someone to talk to, if you need to.

Skyping and texting and writing e's and IMs—all that stuff is cool, and it's good to stay in touch, but nothing comes close to us being together in person, where we can talk about anything and everything, and be there for one another. It was the great gift of boarding school that, somehow, chance brought us together, but love made us—and *keeps* us—best of friends.

TEN

"CLEO! *CLEO!* QUIET," GEORGE COMMANDS FROM the kitchen in Grand's apartment.

Cleo stops barking and lets out a little wheezy sigh instead.

Grand stands in the open French doors to her terrace, wearing an orchid and navy blue print caftan. Her blond hair is up in a turban. She looks like Suzy Parker advertising resort wear in *Vogue* in 1950. I know about Suzy Parker because Grand has a poster of her in her bathroom.

On the terrace, Romy, Suzanne, and Marisol look over midtown Manhattan. Andrew points out the Empire State Building to the girls, while Maurice and Caitlin are huddled on the chaise lounge deep in conversation (as usual).

If I had to choose one of my roommates who looks like she has the potential to become a future New Yorker, it would be Marisol. She takes the city in like a deep breath. She's in awe of the skyscrapers, the subway trains, and the people. Marisol is a people person and we have millions of them, so she's definitely in her glory. She watches the crowds with fascination, as if to remember every detail.

Grand and George have a full house this morning. This is a good practice round for the cast party, where fifty people or more will pack into the apartment. Mom serves coffee to Dad, while Mrs. Santry pours cream into a cup for Mr. Santry.

"Okay, ladies and gentlemen. We've got brioche stuffed French toast . . . ," Grand begins.

"Bacon," George calls out from the kitchen.

"Bacon. Crispy."

"Orange juice," George recommends.

"*Fresh-squeezed* orange juice," Grand says.

"Fruit cup," George adds.

"You heard him," Grand says.

"It sounds delicious, Ms. Cerise," Marisol says politely.

"Please, call me Grand." She smiles.

"Corrie, we're all set." George opens the butler shutters between the living room and the galley kitchen. He places a platter of golden French toast, surrounded by strips of crispy bacon, on the ledge. Then he gives Grand a large cut-crystal bowl of fresh fruit: sliced mango, chunks of sweet cantaloupe, and red grapes. She places the platter and bowl on the coffee table.

"It's a buffet. Plates are on the console."

"Eat up," Mom says.

"You have a big schlep today and you need the fuel." Dad smiles.

"I can't wait to go to the top of the Empire State Building," Marisol says as she helps herself to George's French toast.

"You must," Grand says. "And then, when you watch *An Affair to Remember,* it will mean something to you."

"Deborah Kerr and Cary Grant. Can't beat them. My mother made me watch that movie a hundred times," Mom says.

"And look. It *took*. You grew up and became a film editor," Grand says.

"Do you like old movies?" Mom asks Mr. Santry.

"Not really. My idea of a classic film is *Meatballs* with Bill Murray."

"I'm with you," my dad agrees. "Give me a crowd-pleaser any day."

Dad and Mr. Santry have become good friends very quickly. They really like each other. Usually my dad goes along with whatever friends my mom makes for them as a couple, but friendship with Mr. Santry is all Dad's idea.

"For a filmmaker, my husband has very commercial tastes," Mom explains.

"Nothing wrong with that. Pays the bills." Grand smiles.

"What are your favorite places in Manhattan?" Suzanne asks Grand. "Like, if you were visiting—what would you not want to miss?"

"I'll give them to you in order. Viola, make a list. . . ."

I put down my French toast and flip the lens cap off my camera. "Okay, Grand, fire away."

"These are the places you should not miss in New York City, according to Coral Cerise. . . ." Grand smiles for the camera. I look into the viewfinder. She really is photogenic. Even if she weren't an actress, the camera loves the planes of her face.

Marisol, excellent student that she is, flips open her notebook and writes down a list as I film Grand.

"Number one: the Cloisters. You will think you're in a monastery in France."

"Love the Cloisters," Mom agrees.

"Number two: Central Park Lake. Romantic. Pristine. The arched bridge is to die for. Very Florentine. Very Italian."

"My favorite," Dad says. "I proposed to my wife in a canoe there. And we've been paddling upstream ever since," he jokes.

"Number three," Grand continues. "The Boat Basin at West Seventy-ninth Street."

"I'm with you, Grand. A very boho choice," Andrew says.

"Well, I'm not trying to be au courant, just *interesting*. Let's not choose the same old, same old. Here's why I choose the Boat Basin. There's a sweet restaurant nestled in the underpass, a great jazz spot, but that's not the point. You can get great jazz in the Village. No, it's the little community of boat dwellers that makes it unique. There are a few sturdy New Yorker artist types who choose not to live on dry land in apartments but on their boats year-round, and dock them right there on the pier. It's a fabulous lifestyle choice."

"If you don't mind constant motion," Dad says.

Grand ignores him. "George? Take it away."

Grand removes herself from the shot and George, holding a plate of French toast, speaks to the camera. "Young lovers"—George looks at Maurice and Caitlin—"should always take the Circle Line. You get a three-sixty perspective of Manhattan, and when you ride the top deck, it gives you three hours of bliss, away from civilization, to canoodle as the skyline sails past."

"What if you're not young?" Mrs. Santry asks.

George laughs. "Then I recommend a slow-cooked Italian meal in the Village—at Piccolo Angolo. Four courses in four hours."

"And tell Renato we sent you," Grand says.

George continues, "My favorite place to think is the Hudson River Park on the Charles Street pier. Second favorite: Chinatown for dumplings."

"That's good if you're on an eating tour," Dad pipes up.

"Then, to cultivate your minds: Do not miss the Metropolitan Museum of Art, in particular the Temple of Dendur—you won't believe the indoor pond; the Frick because it was once someone's home and feels like it still; and of course, the Museum of Modern Art because it's hip and fun and cutting edge."

"Mom, how about you?" I turn the camera on my mother.

"I like the Promenade in Brooklyn and the South Street Seaport."

"And my aunt Naira likes to light candles in Saint Patrick's Cathedral even though we are not Catholic," Caitlin adds.

Grand snaps her fingers. "Forgot that one."

"Since we're in midtown, why don't we begin with Central Park?" I say.

"The zoo!" Grand and George say in unison.

"It's not just for kids," Mom says. "But teenagers and . . . up."

"Perfect." I look at the girls, who agree.

I turn my camera off. I look through the French doors. Caitlin and Maurice have slipped out to the terrace and are looking out over the city. They really are star-crossed lovers, even in broad daylight.

I fell in love with Central Park because of Grand. Whenever I would stay the weekend with her, or when Mom and Dad were working, she'd bring me to the park. I loved the jungle gym, the sandbox, and the swings. There are lots of playgrounds inside the park, and Gram would choose a different one each time. And at the end, she would always take me for a ride on the carousel.

As our group trudges through, on the winding trails off 79th Street, my friends get a sense of the size of the park. Andrew points out the puppet theater, a gingerbread house set on a green hillside off the road. "Remember your birthday party at the puppet theater?" Andrew asks.

"I'll never forget it. *Pippi Longstocking* performed with marionettes."

"It was cool," Andrew says.

"And then they let us have pizza and cake in the lobby. And all the characters from past productions, all the puppets, were hanging overhead on the wall. Peter Pan, Cinderella, and Pinocchio."

"You remember everything, don't you?" Andrew says.

"That's because it's the little things that matter." I pick up a long stick and walk with it. We follow the group into the admissions area of the zoo.

"I'm going to take Dad to the lake," Mrs. Santry says to Suzanne.

"I need some romantic time with your mother," Mr. Santry says.

"Okay, TMI and on top of that, *gross*." Suzanne laughs.

Mr. and Mrs. Santry turn off to go down the path to the lake. The summer sun comes through the trees in ribbons of gold. I lift my camera and focus in on the Santrys, filming them as they go down the light-strewn path.

Mrs. Santry pushes Mr. Santry. They laugh. Then Mrs. Santry stops and kneels next to Mr. Santry's chair. He extends his arms to her. She stands, and Mr. Santry pulls her down onto his lap. They kiss.

Usually, when parents kiss or do anything remotely romantic, it's creepy. But this isn't. I am far enough away that this is like an establishing shot of some greater picture, the backdrop of the scene of a life—a family life. It's beautiful, and it seems to be slowing down in real time. I check my shutter speed. No, it has not slowed to a crawl; it's set in real time.

Mrs. Santry gets up and pushes Mr. Santry down the path, until they disappear behind the hill. Without breaking the shot, I slowly pivot to take in the zoo.

Maurice has his arm around Caitlin as they stand on the ticket line. Andrew hangs back a bit as the girls push through to enter the zoo. I flip the camera off.

"You don't want to go to the zoo, do you?" Andrew says softly.

"Not really. I came here so much as a kid I could be a tour guide. But the girls really want to see it."

Marisol hands Andrew and me a ticket each. We follow them into the zoo.

"What do you say we meet back here in an hour?" Maurice says.

"Fine," I tell him.

Marisol, Suzanne, and Romy look at one another.

"Let's go," I tell them. "The otters are hilarious."

The girls fan out and take pictures of the otters, who lounge in the sun on hillsides of rock, and then dive off their cliffs into a deep pool of icy water. The fence around the otters is clear Lucite, so you can see in and underwater.

Andrew and I sit down on the bench and put our feet up.

"We have to ratchet this tour up," Andrew says.

"What are you thinking?"

"Staten Island Ferry."

"Nice choice."

"There's something about the return trip when you're looking at Manhattan from the Jersey side," he says.

"I agree."

"Viola?"

"Yeah?"

Andrew looks away. "Nothing."

"No, what were you going to say?"

"I don't know."

"You must have *some* idea," I persist.

"Not really."

"Okay." I shrug.

"It's just that I don't know how to say it."

"You can tell me anything," I say, poking him in the ribs.

"I know. You're a good listener." Andrew looks at me and smiles.

"Then fire away," I say encouragingly.

"I pick the wrong girls."

"What do you mean?"

"Mel's getting all weird on me."

"Already?" Hmmm, maybe Mel is real.

"Yeah. It's the distance, I guess."

"That, or you don't communicate well with her."

"Could be," he says.

"Well, work on it."

"It's not that easy. It's not like I know what to say."

"Sure you do. You have no problem talking to me."

"Yeah, but that's *you,* Viola. You're not a girl."

"Pardon me?" I sit bolt upright. Defensive.

"No, no, I didn't mean it like that. You aren't a mysterious girl. I've known you all my life, so I get you. It's not easy when it's me, and I'm out there alone and I meet someone new. Mel isn't like you—and I keep hoping that I'll be able to talk to her the way I talk to you."

"It takes time."

"How much?" Andrew asks.

This is one of the things I find annoying about boys in general. They want results and they want them immediately. Important things take time. You can't rush getting to know someone. "It depends. When I was dating Jared, we were mostly quiet at first. Just little things came up—usually something to do with our cameras, or something general about school, his or mine. But then, after a while, we found a lot of common things to share. About our families. Friends. Stuff like that."

"Mel is pretty."

Hearing Andrew compliment another girl, one I don't know, makes me feel a little odd. "Mr. Santry isn't the only one with too much information."

"Sorry. But it's true."

"I'm sure it is. But that doesn't have anything to do with really getting to know a girl. You have to see beyond that, or all you will ever know is that she's . . . attractive. And that's on the surface. Surface stuff is easy. But you already know that."

"It's just that I'd like to find that combination of friend and . . ."

"Pretty?" I fill in the blank for him. This will come in handy when I take the SAT. Filling in the blanks, that is.

"That makes me sound shallow." He looks off at the otters.

I want to say, *It's because you* are, but I resist the easy bait, unlike the otter that leaps six feet into the air for a sardine from the zookeeper. "Oh, Andrew, you're not exactly shallow."

"I'm not?"

"One hot girlfriend from camp who you have nothing in

common with, and yet pursue, doesn't make you shallow."

"What does it make me?" Andrew asks.

"Typical."

"Where are they?" Suzanne surveys the crowd outside the zoo.

"Maurice said they'd meet us in an hour," Marisol reminds us.

"It's now an hour and . . . sixteen minutes," Andrew says.

"This is how it is with them. They have no concept of time," I complain.

"Only of each other," Marisol says. "They have it bad."

"Well, we can't blow our day waiting around for them. What's next?" Romy asks.

"Empire State Building." I look down at the list we pulled together.

"Text them and tell them to meet us in the Village later," Andrew says.

"Where?"

"Tell them to meet us at Shakespeare's on Bleecker."

"Why?"

"I'll be hungry, and you said they were like Romeo and Juliet." Andrew buries his hands in his pockets. "Where else would they eat?"

I text Maurice and give him the specifics. They'll miss the Empire State Building, but it doesn't matter. They have enough reminders of their true love; they don't need a scene from *An Affair to Remember.* Besides, the only view they care about is the one of each other.

"Get the burger," I advise Marisol.

"Okay."

We're at Shakespeare's. Marisol really debates about what to eat. She never just randomly picks a dish. I've found that telling her exactly what to do keeps the day moving forward. The last thing we need as we tour the city is to get bogged down.

We took two tables of four on the street and pushed them together. The waitress is giving us the eye. "Sorry. We're expecting two more people," I explain.

"You'd better text Maurice again," Suzanne says.

I pull out my BlackBerry.

Me: Maurice. Seriously. Get here. We're ordering.

"Okay, I tried. He ignores the texts." I shrug.

"Why?" Romy wants to know.

"He's not checking his BlackBerry," Andrew says. "Trust me."

"How do you know?" Marisol asks.

"Because the only text he wants to answer is one from Caitlin. And he doesn't have to look at his BlackBerry because he's with her," Andrew says.

"What if there's an emergency?" I ask.

"Yeah. Well, there is one, I'm starving." Suzanne studies the menu.

"Hey, don't shoot the messenger. That's how a guy thinks."

"Oh, I'm so excited. I love to watch the gears work in a boy's mind," Romy says.

"It's like looking into a blown lightbulb," I offer.

I sit back and fan myself with the menu. It's a hot afternoon, and as the day has gone on, it's gotten more humid. We've done a lot of running around, a lot of subways.

Mr. and Mrs. Santry enjoyed relaxing by the lake in Central Park. They passed on the ferry and the Empire State Building. Smart. They agreed to meet us back in Brooklyn later. I think they are having a second honeymoon—parents in love, but it's okay. Mr. and Mrs. Santry deserve a little fun.

I love to watch people when I'm sitting at an outdoor café.

The sidewalks are filled with rush hour workers

heading toward the subway station, on their way home. I squint in the distance and see someone familiar. My heart begins to race.

Mrs. Pullapilly comes toward us.

With each step she takes, I realize it isn't a mirage, or a look-alike; it's really *her,* and we're in trouble.

I nudge Andrew, who looks in Mrs. Pullapilly's direction.

When he sees her, he says, "This is bad."

"What?" Suzanne asks. "I shouldn't get the burger?"

"Get whatever you want." But what I really *want* to say is . . . Run!

"Remain calm," Andrew says, in a way that helps me catch my breath as my heart races. But somehow, even his soothing words can't change the situation. No, I have a feeling this is *The Showdown of the Summer of 2010,* and there's no turning back.

ELEVEN

MRS. PULLAPILLY WALKS AT A CLIP TOWARD SHAKE-speare's. Maybe she's going to the bodega for a soda and doesn't even see me, or maybe she's got an appointment around here, business of some sort, or maybe she likes the coffee bean shop that sells exotic beans from South America, and she's just coincidentally in the hood. Right.

I look away from her and search the streets in the opposite direction, hoping to see Caitlin, by some miracle, *without* Maurice. I'm hoping if they took the bus, they'll see us first, and then Mrs. P, and just keep on riding.

Or maybe there is still a way to warn them.

I text Maurice. Again.

Me: Mrs. P at restaurant. Do not come here.

"Did you know she was coming?" Andrew says in my ear.

"No way," I whisper back.

"Maybe Caitlin invited her."

"Look at her face. That's not the expression of a happy mother coming to join her daughter for a hamburger to meet the boyfriend she doesn't know exists. We have to do something."

Mrs. Pullapilly, with her tawny skin and shiny black hair pulled up high in a ponytail, is very beautiful. However, when she's angry, she's *scary,* the opposite of pretty. Her black eyes dart around the street; she looks at the faces of strangers, hoping to find Caitlin's in the crowd.

The wave of panic that shadows Mrs. P's face makes me feel sorry for her for just a moment. It reminds me of when my mom and I got separated at Madison Square Garden at a Norah Jones concert. I could see Mom but she couldn't hear me, and the look on her face was pure panic, just like Mrs. P's is right now.

Andrew places his napkin on the table. "I'll go and find Caitlin and Maurice and head them off."

Mrs. P catches my eye. I wave to her with a big, fake smile. "Too late. She saw me."

"Who?" Suzanne asks.

"Caitlin's mother."

"Whoa," Romy says, piecing together the present moment with all the talks we've had about Caitlin and Maurice and their forbidden cross-cultural, intercontinental romance.

"How does she know we're here?" I say through clenched teeth.

"Mothers have radar," Suzanne whispers.

My roommates can see from my expression that the *worst* possible thing has happened. But they are loyal and they have my back, so they go into smiley/peppy/chatty mode to cover for what I have been forced to hide all summer. Friends are good for that—we are tighter than the basket weave on the leather tote Grand gave me for walking Cleo all summer.

Mrs. P walks right up to our table and plants herself outside the fence line that cordons off the tables from the interior of Shakespeare's and the rest of the sidewalk.

"Hello, Mrs. P!" I chirp.

"Where's Caitlin?" She folds her hands across her chest, as if to contain her anger.

"She's going to meet us here."

"Your mother told me you would be here."

"I'm sure she'll be here any minute." And I hope her boyfriend got the text, I'm thinking.

"Caitlin told me she was going to work today." Mrs. P has slung her briefcase on a long strap across her back. I'm sure the last thing she wanted to do was leave her own work to chase down Caitlin. "Do you know anything about that?"

"No, I'm sorry. I don't," I tell her.

Mrs. P continues, "I went to Dr. Balu's, and he said she took off all of last week and today. But Caitlin didn't tell me."

Andrew gently kicks me under the table to remind me not to volunteer further information. But here's the thing: I had no idea that Caitlin skipped work. It turns out she's been telling me tales too. Either she really loves Maurice or she is determined to be shipped back to India for their version of convent school. Either way, this isn't good. But maybe all is not lost, maybe Mrs. P doesn't know everything. Mrs. P has a lot of facts, but she's also fishing. I'm going to do my best to continue to cover for Caitlin.

"Oh, well, see, my roommates are in town, and we invited her to come with us to tour the city. Maybe she forgot. . . ."

Mrs. Pullapilly's eyes narrow. "Caitlin does not

forget. Where is she now?"

"We were at the zoo. She said she was going to meet us here." I try to sound breezy.

"You left her alone in the park?" Mrs. P's eyes narrow even more.

My roommates, especially Marisol, begins to crack under this pressure. Marisol looks around and tries to smooth over the situation. "She should be here any minute."

Andrew stands.

"Sit down, Andrew," Mrs. Pullapilly says. "It's too late. You cannot warn her."

"Warn her?" He sits back down.

"I know about the boy," Mrs. Pullapilly says.

"The boy?" Andrew acts surprised at the mention of a boy.

"The British boy. Dr. Balu's assistant told me that he waits for her after work, and that he has been there every day for weeks. That was, of course, when she was still showing up for work."

"Oh, Dr. Balu has it all wrong," I tell her. "We're all just friends. The whole group of us. Maurice is the son of the Broadway director who's in charge of Grand's play."

"Oh, so Caitlin hasn't been seeing this boy alone?"

"No. I see more of him than she does."

"Of course, he lives at the apartment at the Chestertons'," Marisol says.

I give her a look that says, *Not helpful*.

Mrs. Pullapilly places her hands on her hips. She shifts her weight from one foot to the other as if to count the moments until Caitlin and Maurice arrive and my lie blows up like the steam coming out of the manhole on Greene Street.

"Viola, I'm very disappointed in you. When you lie for someone, it is worse than doing the bad deed."

My roommates look at one another. I'm embarrassed. I want to say something, but I can't. Instead, my throat closes and tears sting my eyes. I quickly wipe the tears away.

Mrs. P could care less that I feel bad. She is so angry I could see her standing on the sidewalk for *hours* until Caitlin shows up. She turns around and cranes her neck to look over the crowd, hoping to see her daughter. Then she turns back to us.

We all feel guilty as we sit in silence.

I look at Andrew, whose eyes widen as he focuses on Bleecker Street. Quickly, he reads the menu as if to study it, but it is too late. Mrs. P caught his reflection in the window and saw that Andrew noticed *something*. So she moves to the end of the fence, and at last, she sees

Caitlin and Maurice, arm in arm, walking toward the restaurant. Her face goes to sheer relief and then back to stoic anger in three seconds flat.

Caitlin and Maurice do not see Mrs. Pullapilly. As usual, they are in their own world, with eyes, ears, and hearts only for each other.

My stomach churns as Mrs. P gets a good eyeful of what I've been seeing all summer. Caitlin's face is the picture of pure happiness, and Maurice is in bliss. Even if they wanted to hide their true feelings, it would be impossible.

As Caitlin and Maurice enter the fenced area of the restaurant, Caitlin sees us at our table and waves to us. Then she sees her mother. Caitlin's face is stricken with fear. She quickly removes her arm from around Maurice's waist, but he does not remove his from hers (worse!).

"Caitlin. Come here. *Now,*" Mrs. P says loudly. Her voice echoes through the café. Heads turn.

Maurice is confused, until he lays eyes on Mrs. Pullapilly, and then he gets it. Caitlin pivots and comes out of the fenced-in area and joins her mother on the sidewalk. Maurice turns to follow her, and she turns back to him and says, "No."

Maurice honors Caitlin's request, but he's not happy about it. I try to stand up to explain what is going on, but Suzanne pulls me back down into my seat.

Mrs. Pullapilly takes Caitlin by the elbow, and without a good-bye, she hustles her down the street, back to the subway. I watch them disappear down the stairs.

"That woman!" Maurice is furious.

"Caitlin's been skipping work?"

"So?"

"So, Dr. Balu narced. And Mrs. Pullapilly is furious."

"I'll just explain everything to Mrs. Pullapilly," Maurice says.

"It's too late! She knows we lied. That's the last time you'll see Caitlin. Mrs. Pullapilly will see to it."

"And Caitlin will see to it that we *do*." Maurice practically sneers.

"Good luck," I tell him. Maurice is stubborn, superior, and in a strange way, exactly like Mrs. Pullapilly. "Not happening," I tell him.

"She'll run away with me," he says.

I throw my hands up. "Now *there's* a plan. Maurice, you're going back to England. Caitlin has school—and no electronics, no BlackBerry, no phone, except the one her parents gave her—and they check it. She barely emails unless it's schoolwork. How did you think this was going to work?"

"Love finds a way," Maurice says.

I make a mental note that boys, when confronted about anything, respond with a catch-all phrase that describes their feelings, instead of actually saying what they're feeling. Very annoying.

"You never know. Maybe Mrs. Pullapilly will calm down and listen to reason," Romy says.

"Dream on." Suzanne snaps a breadstick in half and bites it.

"I think it's the heat." Romy fans herself. "A little."

"We're not doing anything wrong," Maurice says defensively.

"Maurice, you don't get it," Andrew says calmly. "Caitlin is allowed to hang with us because her parents trust Viola and me. We've earned their trust."

"It took us *years*," I assure Maurice.

"I'm going to go and explain this to the Pullapillys." Maurice gets up and walks toward the subway.

"Maurice!" I call after him, but he ignores me.

The food comes, but I can't eat. I feel horrible for Caitlin. She was actually beginning to be a normal teenager this summer. We could see signs that the Pullapillys trusted her and that things were changing. Andrew and I felt welcome in their home. Mrs. P was great about letting Caitlin come with Andrew and me to Mermaid Day and into the city. Now all the good will we built has been ruined.

This is all my fault. I knew this would end in disaster. I know Caitlin and her family; I should have insisted that Caitlin tell her mom and dad that she liked Maurice and hoped to spend time with him. After all, they welcome Andrew into their home and he's a boy. Maybe they would have done the same with Maurice.

I should have listened to my mother! I knew there was trouble ahead when Caitlin and Andrew rode off in the train the night they were supposed to have dinner with me.

They seemed doomed to me, even then. As for opening night on Broadway, the plans I made with my roomies and my homies were just too good to be true. What were the chances that Grand would have a show opening on Broadway and that I would be able to host all my friends *together* for one night? This opportunity will never come our way again. I was determined to merge my life from Prefect with my life in Brooklyn. Sometimes when you get exactly what you want, it's the worst possible thing that could happen.

What a summer.

Andrew miss-kissed me, Caitlin was taken prisoner, and my roomies' vacation to NYC turned into a major drama. Maybe this is what happens when you turn fifteen. We're too young to do what we want, and too old to ask permission for every little thing.

Suzanne, Romy, and Marisol gather around the Avid in my parents' office.

"Okay, remember, this is just raw footage," I remind them.

I hit Play and run the video.

Scenes from their visit roll out in all their summer beauty.

The girls laugh at their arrival in Bay Ridge.

Andrew hams it up on the Staten Island Ferry. I got an excellent angle on the Statue of Liberty as we passed. I held the shot steady as the waves on the Hudson River jostled us.

The panoramic sweep from the top of the Empire State Building is magnificent. The clear blue sky behind the black and gray buildings is a palette from a painting.

The zoo footage is hilarious. A seal practically snaps Marisol's hand off when she tries to feed him a sardine. I lined up the girls on the swings and shot them swinging in a row. The most beautiful shots of the bridge and the lake in Central Park are poignant because of Mr. and Mrs. Santry. You can see how much they love each other. The lighting was just right, a soft peach tone, to capture the summer day.

I have a lot to work with.

"Well, it's a start," I tell them.

"Are you kidding? It's already fabulous," Marisol says.

"It will be, once I make a story out of it."

"You get better every time you film something," Romy marvels.

"Thanks."

Suzanne doesn't say anything. Marisol, Romy, and I look to her. She stares at the screen, and at the image of her dad and mom, frozen on the lake in Central Park. They are in a canoe. Without the wheelchair, Mr. Santry looks completely normal—any man and his wife on the lake on a summer day.

Romy looks at me. Marisol nudges me. I take the hint.

"Okay, who needs ice cream?" I say.

"Let's go!" Romy says.

We grab Suzanne and head down the stairs to the kitchen. It's important to be happy when you can be, because as surely as we're having fun, we know that sadness is lurking around the corner like a night shadow.

Grand says it's true of the craft of acting, and just living: *Stay in the moment.*

It's the morning of opening night. I wake up with butterflies in my stomach. I can only imagine Grand and George and Mary Pat Gleason and the rest of the cast.

They must be nervous wrecks.

My roomies are exhausted and sleeping in. Walking New York City from the Apollo Theater to Wall Street really wore them out. I'm used to the long walks because of Cleo. I think I built up some leg muscles this summer.

I tiptoe out of my room, careful not to wake them.

Mom called Mrs. Pullapilly, to try to explain my side of things, but to no avail. Maurice has not left the apartment downstairs, and it looks like he is going to skip opening night altogether, unless, of course, I can figure something out.

I go down the front stairs, and down the hallway to the kitchen. Mr. Santry is having breakfast. Mrs. Santry is making toast.

"Good morning."

Mr. Santry looks up from the newspaper. "Your face says the opposite of 'good morning.'"

"Still no word from Caitlin?" Mrs. Santry asks.

"Nope." I pour myself a cup of orange juice and sit down at the table with them. "I'm sorry that you came to New York and endured the Caitlin and Maurice version of *West Side Story*."

"That would have been entertaining. The real thing, not so much." Mr. Santry looks at me. "We feel bad for you. For everybody."

"Is there anything we can do?" Mrs. Santry asks.

"I don't think so. Mom called, and it didn't do a bit of good."

"You know her parents will eventually forgive Caitlin," Mr. Santry says.

"Yeah, maybe. In twenty years. I had no idea Caitlin was lying about work. I think that's what hurt Mrs. Pullapilly the most. The boyfriend is bad enough, but being irresponsible with her summer job? They really don't go for that. But she just wanted time with Maurice."

"Well, it's difficult." Mrs. Santry looks at her husband. "When you're in the midst of a crush or a new love, whatever you want to call it, reason goes out the window. That's why we've told our sons and our daughter that you need to think when you meet someone new—don't get caught up. I think that Caitlin and Maurice heard the ticking of the clock. . . ."

"And it was a bomb."

Mr. Santry laughs. "What my wife is saying is that Caitlin and Maurice acted impulsively. Caitlin should have gone to her mother."

"I asked her to do that."

"And if she asked her mother's permission and her mother said no, see, Caitlin would have had to abide by that."

"Caitlin didn't ask her mom because there is no way her mother would have let her have *one* date, let alone—a daily date for six weeks."

"We get it," Mrs. Santry says.

"Viola, I think you should try to talk to Mrs. Pullapilly. The opening of a Broadway play is a big deal—and Caitlin should be with her friends tonight."

"You think she might hear me out?"

"If you go to her with respect and if you stay calm, you might be surprised at how she responds." Mr. Santry smiles.

If I ever needed extra parents, and I don't, I think I would choose the Santrys. Maybe because they had sons first, they have a very honest and open way of dealing with girl-boy relationships. The Santrys are reasonable parents.

Caitlin is the eldest in her family, and she's like a second mother to her brother and sister. It's almost as though Mrs. P expects Caitlin to be mature when it comes to work, chores, and responsibilities, but stay twelve years old when it comes to boys. Caitlin is a great student, but she has to rank first in academics, violin, sports, and virtue. Who could live up to the pressure?

No, give me the Santrys. They're realistic. They let Suzanne work at the Dairy Queen, they don't scare her about boys, and they advise her without making her feel like an idiot. *They help her.*

Mom calls the Santry family "True Midwesterners." She says it with respect, like being a Midwesterner is something to aim for. I think of pioneers, farms, and hard work when I think of the Midwest. They're solid people with good values, but that's not why I like them. I like them because they're real and don't act like every problem is the end of the world. I need to learn this kind of calm. After all, I'm a Brooklyn girl with a grandmother who is an actress. We know how to press the drama button.

TWELVE

I FILM THE ENTRANCE OF 116 PROSPECT STREET, then the sign over the door: THE METROPOLITAN INSURANCE AGENCY. I flip on the sound. "Video diary, take note. I am outside Mrs. Pullapilly's office. When I turn the camera off, I will go inside. And I will hopefully see Mrs. P and explain my side of the story regarding Caitlin. How will it turn out?"

I flip off the camera. Whenever I have a challenge, a test, or a tense situation, I often record myself *before* I have to do the very thing that scares me. This certainly qualifies as one of those moments.

I slip the camera back into the case. I sign in at the front desk and head for the elevator to the seventh floor. I have an instinct with each step to just turn and run.

After all, I know what awaits me—and it isn't pretty.

When I get to the seventh floor, the receptionist is gone. I check the sign for the names of the employees. I find Mrs. P in suite 701. I push through the glass doors and look for 701.

I knock softly on Mrs. Pullapilly's office door.

"Come in," she says from inside.

I push the walnut door open. Mrs. Pullapilly's office overlooks the East River. Her decor is homey, yet professional. "Hi, Mrs. Pullapilly."

She looks up at me, and her stern expression softens a little. People who can be scary sometimes know it, and she knows she scares me. "How are you, Viola?"

"I'm okay." I force a smile. Then I remember my manners. "How are you?"

"I'm okay," she says.

"Well, I guess you know why I'm here."

"Do I?" she says softly.

"I came to talk to you about Maurice and Caitlin."

"It's not really any of your business." She smiles tensely.

"But it is. We're all friends. And now that's been ruined."

"Caitlin lied to me, and we do not stand for that in our home."

"Nobody does, Mrs. Pullapilly."

"You were part of the lie, Viola."

"And I'm very sorry," I tell her.

"I accept your apology," Mrs. Pullapilly says.

We sit in silence for a moment. Mrs. Pullapilly taps her pen on her desk and looks down.

"I was just being loyal. Mrs. P, they are not criminals. They just like to be together. They had a spark from the first moment."

"It's not possible for Caitlin."

"They really care for each other."

"I don't question that, Viola."

"I think I might understand some things about liking a boy. I can see liking a boy, and wanting to spend time with him, if he was good and kind and smart. You must have liked Mr. P when you met him."

Mrs. P actually smiles for the first time since the restaurant. "It's different."

"Maurice isn't from India, but he's a good guy."

"I'm sure he's very nice. But the circumstances are not. Caitlin has great potential. My mother warned me when we moved here that the United States is permissive, and that would eventually cause me problems. And it has. She was right. Listen to your mother."

"But this isn't about permissiveness, or American

culture—it's about Caitlin. She's a very good person. She is a loving friend. You wouldn't want her to give up the violin because somebody banned the instrument. It's the same with someone's heart. If a girl has a passion for music, it's possible she might also love field hockey, or chemistry or . . . sometimes . . . even a boy."

Mrs. Pullapilly looks out the window. I think she took in what I said, but with parents, it's often hard to tell.

"It doesn't matter anyway, Viola. Maurice is going back to England, and Caitlin will go back to school."

I take a deep breath. At least the Pullapillys aren't going to send Caitlin to India for school. "So . . . love can't find her if they are continents apart."

"Exactly correct." Mrs. P finally agrees with me.

"I'm sorry I was part of the deception."

"I was very surprised that you were. I trusted you, Viola."

I get up and go to the door. Then I turn and face Mrs. Pullapilly.

"He's just a boy, Mrs. Pullapilly." I take a breath. "Will you reconsider allowing Caitlin to come to the play tonight? My grandmother has tickets for you and Mr. Pullapilly, too."

"We were very happy to be included. But circumstances have changed, and we won't be able to make it."

Once I'm out on the street, I flip on the camera and turn the lens back toward the building. "I have the answer to how the meeting with Mrs. Pullapilly went. Not well. Not well at all."

My bedroom on opening night reminds me of our quad at Prefect when all four of us were getting ready to go out. Blow-dryers whirl, music blares, and there is a lot of shouting and peals of the kind of laughter that begets more laughter. Trying to put on makeup when you're laughing is impossible. Also, trying to put on makeup only to look like we're not wearing any (or too much) is, frankly, absurd.

We have our quirks when it comes to dressing up.

Marisol always tries on twelve variations of one outfit. (Leggings? No. Skirt and leggings? Maybe. Blouse tucked in? No. Out? Yes? Belted?) For every outfit Marisol tries on, Romy does the same with her hairdo. (Up, down, braid, loose, side part, center part, no part. Curlers? No. Flatiron? Yes.)

I agonize about shoes: yellow flats or blue patent platforms, espadrilles or closed shoes? It isn't just a fashion choice to me, but an actual statement of where I'm going. I have a lot of shoes because I like to cover a lot of ground.

Suzanne, unlike Marisol, Romy, or me, puts out minimal effort when it comes to wardrobe, hair, makeup, and accessories. She has the same approach whenever we glam up for a special night. Suzanne disappears to go for a run, or grabs a snack, or takes her laptop to read the news online or answer emails. Then, in the final moments, just before it's time to go, she breezes in, throws on a dress and flats, anchors a hair band to her head, checks the look in the mirror, and is done. The results are exactly right. Without any stress at all, Suzanne looks like she lives in a Ralph Lauren bubble blown by Kate Spade.

Mom pokes her head in the door. "Looking good, girls."

Marisol whistles at Mom.

"Mom, you look amazing," I tell her.

Mom is wearing a white sleeveless dress with silver spangles along the hem. She wears silver strappy sandals on her feet. Her hair has highlights (from the salon, not the box), and she wears pink lipstick. "Thank you," she says. "Everybody's ready downstairs."

The girls grab their purses, and we file out of my room and follow Mom down the stairs. I grab my camera and quickly flip it on. I get a nice shot of the girls and Mom going down the front stairs.

Mom wears a perfume called Coco, and the scent of jasmine and lilies trails behind her like a summer bouquet.

Andrew is in the foyer, wearing a suit (he had a lot of weddings in his family this year, so his dad took him to Syms and bought him one). He looks handsome. If he wasn't my BFFAA, I would think he was a catch.

"Is something wrong?" Andrew asks, when he spots me staring at him.

"Your tie is crooked," I tell him.

"Well, fix it."

I fix Andrew's tie, and for a moment, we're back on the roof when he kissed me. I step back and remember how that kiss practically shipwrecked our entire friendship.

"Thanks," Andrew says, checking his tie in the hallway mirror.

Mr. Santry is in his wheelchair. He and Dad are wearing tuxedos. Mrs. Santry looks beautiful in a long dress the color of eggplant. She wears turquoise shoes and carries a matching purse. Mom holds her purse while she fixes Mr. Santry's bow tie.

I go in for a close-up and catch Mrs. Santry making Mr. Santry laugh as she adjusts the bow tie and then smooths his lapels.

I widen out and include my roomies in the shot.

"Well, look at the lovely ladies," Dad says. "Andrew, you are a lucky fellow."

All five of us turn shades of red from pale pink (Suzanne) to fuchsia (Romy). Nothing worse than my dad sounding like a Vegas opening act when referring to my friends and me.

Dad arranged for a minibus to take us into the city. We follow Mom and Mrs. Santry down the front steps. Dad and Andrew help Mr. Santry down the ramp in his wheelchair. My parents and I were worried about getting Mr. Santry around the city, but we haven't had a problem. Everyone pitches in and helps. Sometimes Mr. Santry seems concerned that he is a bother because he needs help, but we joke him out of it.

I film our group as they load into the minibus. Once we're inside, I take a slow pan of the street through the window.

"Bridge or tunnel?" the driver says.

"Bridge!" we holler.

As we sail across the Brooklyn Bridge, the sun begins to set, far in the west, behind Manhattan, and beyond New Jersey. In the foreground, the sky over the city turns lavender with streaks of orange. The skyscrapers turn a dull silver in the setting sun.

The cables suspended over the Brooklyn Bridge look like the threads of a spiderweb in the light. Twilight sets the perfect mood for opening night. There is a feeling of promise, and the hope of magic to come.

"What happened to Maurice?" Romy asks as she adjusts the spaghetti straps of her dress with her thumbs.

"He ended up going into the city with his dad earlier."

"So he's coming to the show after all?" Suzanne asks.

"His dad made him."

"He *should* go. After all, he interned for his dad," Marisol says practically.

"I don't think Maurice is in the mood to do anything but mope."

"Viola, did Caitlin ever call you?"

"No. I think I made it worse going to see her mother."

"It was the right thing to do," Suzanne says. "You needed to explain what really happened."

"Well, I did do that. But I don't think she liked what I had to say."

"There are times when no explanation will do." Andrew checks the light gauge on my camera. "You tried, Vi. You reached out to her, and it didn't get you the result you wanted. But you know—you were always friends with Caitlin, and you always will be. Once schools starts, maybe things will get back to normal."

I don't know why I do this, but when I feel bad, I think about things that actually make me feel worse. I want to have a wonderful time tonight, but somehow, it won't be as good without Caitlin. And even though I found Maurice and her a bit much this summer, with the hand holding and the whispering, I never wanted to see either of them unhappy. And somehow, I blame myself for all of this. I knew what would happen if Mrs. P found out about Maurice, and I just didn't do enough to stop the inevitable.

One of the things I learned at boarding school was that sometimes you just have to let things play out. Jared Spencer showed signs of being a dork, but I didn't break it off right away, because, let's face it, *anybody* can be a dork depending on the situation, including me. So, instead of ending my relationship with Jared when I saw signs that it might not work, I let it play out. I did the same thing with my idea for my first film. I didn't know where it was going, but I wrote the script, and once I got it on its feet, the actors (Grand and George) helped me find the spine of the thing. And when I'm editing footage, I often think to cut away from something because it seems repetitive or not very interesting, but if I leave it there for a while, the answer comes, and I figure out how to make it work, or in the end, I cut it. But I never go in there like Edward Scissorhands and hack the piece into a shape that appears pleasing just to finish. I wait it out.

Caitlin's mom couldn't see that she needed to let things play out. Mrs. P is not that type of mother or person. She has a plan in place. Any deviation from that plan is interpreted as defiance, and that does not fly in any fashion in the Pullapilly home. I almost wish Caitlin had a year at Prefect, to get her sea legs and make some decisions on her own. Maybe then, Mrs. Pullapilly would see that Caitlin is intelligent and has good sense.

The minibus pulls up to the front of the theater. First, the driver helps Mr. Santry out, with a small ramp attached to the running board. Then we pile out. Andrew waits for the girls to exit. He's the last one out. I flip on the camera and begin to film the Opening Crowd.

A strong beam of sunset light pours from the west onto 44th Street. There is a lot of upbeat chatter, and the audience is dressed for opening night. A lot of dazzling sequins, end-of-summer dresses, ruffles, and tuxedos. I take a deep breath. Of all the things I have loved about Grand's opening nights through the years, it's the scents of ladies' perfumes, all mingled together, like the whoosh you get in the rare flower room at the New York Botanical Garden in the Bronx. It's heady, it's clean, and it's completely exotic. It's almost as if the theater becomes an enchanted island, complete with the breeze of the scent of rare flowers.

Mom hands us our tickets.

"You guys can hang out here. We're early," she says, smiling at us. She turns to follow the Santrys and my dad into the theater. Then she turns back to me. She leans in, puts her hand on my face, and whispers in my ear, "I know you miss Caitlin. But let's have fun."

I nod that I will try. Mom follows the crowd into the ticket line, which is moving quickly to let people into their seats.

"Let's get a shot from across the street," Andrew says.

Andrew and I wait for some traffic to pass. We run across the street. From the uptown side, we film the facade of the Helen Hayes Theatre. I think about Grand inside, who has been ready for a few hours. She has walked through her cues onstage, put on her wig, stepped into her dress and shoes, and now is moments away from being an old, funny, dotty lady, Aunt Martha.

"Here," Andrew says, taking the camera. He lifts it and gets a nice shot of the marquee. "Viola?"

"Yeah?" I look up at Andrew.

Andrew says, "You look pretty."

"Thanks. So do you."

Andrew looks as if he wants to say something more, but he doesn't.

"I'm glad you're home," I tell him.

"It was a long year without you," he says.

"It may be a long year with me, Andrew. You're about to find out."

We laugh and cross the street, joining Romy and Suzanne and Marisol. "Is it time?" Romy says, excited.

"This is it." I place my camera in the leather tote Grand gave me, burying it under a sleeve of chamois cloth. I pull out my ticket. "Ready, guys?"

We line up to go into the theater. Once inside, I realize Marisol is not with us. I look out the door and see her on the sidewalk, taking it all in. She stands in the last beams of the setting August sun, and I swear, for a moment, if she could fly, she would. She'd sail over the city and between the tips of the skyscrapers with only the light from the windows and streetlamps to guide her. Marisol has fallen in love with New York City, and she's got it *bad*.

"Marisol!" I shout.

She turns and looks at me.

"Let's go."

She smiles and gets on the line with us. I love that we get to sit in the first row. Mom, Dad, Mrs. Santry, and

Mr. Santry (whose chair tucks in nicely into a gap on the aisle) sit in the center of the orchestra, in the second row.

We take our seats and programs and look up at the grand curtain, which is covered with images of berries made by gobos over the lighting instruments. The berries are inspired by the ingredients used to make poisonous elderberry wine. Julius Ross designed his own patterns and cut them into the metal squares so the audience would be greeted by the exact right image. Julius may be a temperamental artist, and a man who ran me all over the city on crazy errands, but he's also a brilliant lighting designer, which makes up for his impatience and trying personality.

Maurice slips into the empty aisle seat next to me.

"You okay?" I whisper.

"Horrid."

"I'm sorry, Maurice."

"I miss her," he says.

"So do I."

"I tried to talk to her parents."

"So did I."

"They told me it wasn't possible for me to see her."

"It's awful."

"You know what is the worst thing of all?" Maurice turns to me.

"What?"

"I really adore her. Really and truly. I would never hurt her. And somehow, her parents believe that I will."

"It's not you, Maurice. It would be any boy that she liked."

"That doesn't make it any easier. Every person wants to be seen for who they truly are. Not some silly idea of what they think you are."

The curtain rises to the wah-wah music of the 1930s that Mr. Longfellow played until we all wanted to scream. But somehow, in the dark theater, the old-fashioned music hits exactly the right notes and strikes exactly the right mood.

I turn and look up at the follow-spot operators who stand at the ready like fighter pilots. The curtain lifts, and the Brewster living room in Brooklyn comes to life. Afternoon shadows grace the vintage wallpaper. All the levels of the set, the stairs, the upstage windows, the downstage floor, the alcove where the bodies are kept inside an antique bench, are illuminated with exacting pools of light to portend the antics of the black comedy to come.

The opening-night audience bursts into applause when Grand and Mary Pat Gleason mix their brew downstage as the play begins.

George Dvorsky enters, and the women in the audience take in a breath. I memorize every detail so I can tell Caitlin about it later. She will be so sad to have missed it.

I look across the aisle at Mom and Dad and the Santrys. Mr. Santry has propped his elbows on the handles of his wheelchair and leans in, to catch every word. He is in the moment.

I realize that I've been holding my breath from nerves for Grand. By the time the third scene of the first act comes around, I'm able to relax. Andrew places his hand on mine, and that makes me feel better. I look up at him, but Andrew keeps his eyes on the play.

I thread my fingers through his and hold his hand tightly. He smiles and gives my hand a squeeze. I feel a pang of the excitement I felt when Jared Spencer held my hand for the first time.

How crazy is that?

The evening goes by so fast (that's the sign of a good director of comedy) that it leaves us all wanting more. When it comes time for the curtain call, Grand blows kisses to us, and Mom carries a large bouquet of roses to the foot of the stage. Grand gives a deep bow of appreciation. The giant bouquet breaks into four pieces, so each of the women in the cast get a bouquet. The curtain call is long, and the wolf whistles and bravos and bravas don't stop.

Grand looks up and seems to take in the faces of every single person in the audience. Her smile is wide, and her blue eyes sparkle in the beams of light, and only I would know it, but she is so happy, she tries not to cry. But after the second standing ovation, she can't help it. The tears fill her eyes, as the joy of being in a hit at long last fills her heart. As the curtain is lowered, I see George take Grand into his arms and kiss her.

THIRTEEN

THE STAGE MANAGER LETS US UP TO GRAND'S dressing room after the show. We peel through the post-show pandemonium, crew sweeping up and putting props back where they belong, costumers carrying out clothes to be pressed for the next performance.

Andrew decides to wait for us downstairs, so it's just us girls. Mom and Dad will go up later; they're staying on the stage with the Santrys to meet and greet the cast.

There's a crowd of people waiting to get upstairs outside the stage door, but somehow, they let us up first. I get out the camera and take in the opening-night frenzy.

The girls have little gifts for Grand and Mary Pat. Romy brought two jars of elderberry jam, Suzanne has two sets of antique lace doilies, and Marisol has brought them two Mexican voodoo dolls to get rid of bad energy.

We hear Grand and Mary Pat laughing behind the door when I knock.

"Come in!" Grand says.

We push it open. Mary Pat lets out a low wolf whistle. "Look at these gorgeous girls."

"Thank you," we say in unison. "Grand, you and Mary Pat were spectacular," I add.

"Can you believe it?" Grand takes my hands. "We made it."

"Everybody loved it! "

Grand gets tears in her eyes. "What did you think of George?"

My roomies swoon. "He's beautiful!" Romy blurts.

"I agree," Grand says.

Mary Pat is dressed in a chic black sequined pant outfit for the opening-night party. "Hey, kids, I gotta book. I got a hot date." She grabs her purse. "Not as hot as yours, Coral, but pretty darn close."

Mary Pat goes. The girls look around the room with awe. This is the first time they've ever been behind the scenes of a Broadway show.

"Go on, girls. Nose around. George's dressing room is one flight down," Grand says. We turn to go. Grand grabs my arm to stay. I sit down next to her as she removes her stage makeup with a soufflé cream of coconut that Gram can only find in England.

"What do you think? Really?" Grand asks.

"Grand, you were brilliant."

"Thank you, honey. George is something, isn't he?"

"Grand, he loves you so much."

"I wasn't expecting that kiss." She smiles.

"He's so proud of you."

"I can't believe it took me this long to find a man who roots for me in every way. But George does. It amazes me every day."

"Grand, does it bother you that . . ."

"He's the leading man and I play an old lady?" Grand brushes her coral lipstick (of course) over her lips for just a hint of fresh color. "Viola, I could not care less. It's the theater. It's make-believe. What is real always stays real, and what is pretend, well, it stays at the Helen Hayes Theatre. The wigs, the costumes, the sets, and the lights make a world, and we leave it behind. When we come back the next day to tell the story all over again, it's waiting here for us. But this world has no impact on real life. This is the fun stuff. George and I are solid. Don't worry."

"I won't. He's family." I give my grandmother a hug.

"He is, isn't he?" Grand smiles as though this is a

revelation. I guess it never occurs to her that sometimes, love stays. Forever.

Cleo is truly a party animal (not). She sleeps in her cushy cage under Grand's dressing table in the bedroom, oblivious to the noise, music, and din.

After the pre-bash at the Marriott Marquis, which was hosted by Daryl Roth—who now, in Grand's eyes, is up there with Mrs. Obama as a role model—the real party began at Grand's apartment.

My roomies laugh and squeeze through the crowd. Each room is filled to the brim with theater types, actors, crew members, playwrights, and designers. There are small animated huddles of discussion going on throughout the apartment. The terrace is packed with smokers. Grand and George flit around the kitchen, putting out trays of "Italian a-go-go finger food" (as Grand calls it).

Baskets of fresh garlic knots, crackers, and breadsticks; trays of lush roasted peppers, marinated mushrooms, salami, provolone, and olives; and small cups of cold pasta salad arrabiata-style, hot cheese puffs, and shrimp cocktail are gobbled up as fast as George can put them out. And there's plenty.

The desserts, including miniature cannoli, tricolor cookies, and almond and chocolate biscotti, are stacked on polished silver trays on the server.

The hum of the blender is heard in the background as Grand mixes up daiquiris as fast as the guests can down them.

"This party is wild," Romy says, her eyes widening as she takes in the banter and laughter.

"The actors are so different offstage." Marisol watches as Mary Pat Gleason does her best impression of Susan Boyle winning *Britain's Got Talent*. Mary Pat looks years younger without the gray wig. Grand is closer in age to the aunts, but neither of them, offstage, look anything like their characters.

Mr. Santry is holding court by the sofa with a group of playwrights. You can always tell the playwrights. They scowl. The men look like college professors, and the women, harried mothers on their way to the park. The women playwrights tend to wear flowy scarves and sensible shoes, but this is just my snapshot observation.

Andrew is filming a group arguing in the bedroom about union wages breaking the back of producing shows on Broadway. I flip on my camera and take in Mr. Santry and the playwrights as they discuss the dilemma of the written word going forward in a technological age. I'm hoping I can pick up some of the conversation.

Everybody sounds brilliantly smart in this huddle.

The doorbell rings. Mr. Santry checks his watch and looks to the door, so I follow his gaze with the camera. (This is a technique my father taught me when shooting documentaries. Move the camera with the point of view of the subject, and almost always, you will be surprised at the reveal.)

As the door opens, I am not only surprised at the reveal, I am:

Shocked.

Stunned.

Amazed.

Blown away.

Mr. and Mrs. Pullapilly enter the living room, with Caitlin between them. I nearly drop the camera, but record Mr. Santry, who greets the Pullapillys. Caitlin looks at me and smiles. It is a loaded smile, full of meaning. Her expression says, *I'm sorry, I'm happy, and . . . I'm redeemed.*

Mom and Dad see the Pullapillys and go to them. Andrew works his way through the crowd to Caitlin. We give her a good, long group embrace.

"What happened?" I ask Caitlin quietly.

"You went to see my mom, and whatever you said made a difference." Caitlin gets tears in her eyes.

"Viola always knows the exact right thing to say," Andrew says.

"I tried to remind them that you've always done the right thing. And that you always will."

Caitlin gives me a hug. "I'm sorry for all the trouble I caused you."

"It's all fine now, Caitlin," I assure her.

Maurice and Mr. Longfellow come out of the kitchen. They've been watching through the butler window. Maurice joins us. He greets Caitlin with a respectful kiss on the cheek. Maurice turns to the Pullapillys and introduces his father. Grand brings fizzy seltzer for them and introduces herself.

I see my roomies standing across the room, thrilled for Caitlin.

There could not be a better ending to the best opening night in the history of my life. Sometimes, your greatest hopes go unrealized. Grand has always said that about her boyfriends (and husbands), that when you're dewy eyed, you start out with the best of intentions, and things just don't work out. But then there are moments like these, when things actually *do*.

I flip on my camera and step back for a better view of the Pullapillys, the Santrys, and the Chestertons. I hear Mr. Pullapilly talk about the great theater in India, and how the community comes together to make plays, parables really, stories of life in the community. Dad listens closely, while Mom and Mrs. Pullapilly talk about our school, and how happy they are that we are focusing on the arts at LaGuardia.

And Caitlin and Maurice, out of the shadow of hiding their feelings, are actually free. When I look over at Caitlin's parents, I see they are happy too. The truth is out in the open, and no matter where you're from, that's a good thing.

Here are two people, Caitlin and Maurice, who like each other, and found each other in a summer that neither will ever forget. We learned the hard lessons, but we also are celebrating the joy that comes from a chance meeting on a rooftop in Bay Ridge. I don't think, as long as I live, that I will ever forget that night. The sky seemed to change when fate stepped in, and there was no moon because Caitlin and Maurice didn't need one. There was enough light to see who they were to become to each other. And enough to light the path of true love.

The whir of the Lasko fan is the only sound in Bay Ridge. It's three o'clock in the morning, and the quad can't sleep. We are too excited.

"My first Broadway play." Marisol sighs.

"I got five pictures of just me and George," Romy says. "Why do I always go for the unattainable?"

"You're an athlete. Every time you kick a soccer ball, you're thinking about the Olympics," I tell her.

"Right, right," she agrees.

"Viola, if I ever get in a jam with my parents, I'm sending you in to sort it out."

"I had no idea I got through to Mrs. Pullapilly."

"Wow. It worked," Marisol says.

"And now they can be friends across an ocean," I say.

"How romantic," Suzanne says. "Maybe someday they will be together again."

"Maybe." I wonder.

The whir of the fan lulls us to sleep, one by one. I am the last to turn over. There in the dark, I think about how Romy, Suzanne, and Marisol get me through. And how we all blended together, Andrew and Caitlin and my roomies—and even Maurice, who just by chance came into our lives and into our street-level apartment.

Chance really is a big part of what happens in life.

Andrew held my hand during the play—and I remember how that calmed me down. I am lucky to be surrounded by such great friends. That, I guess, in the end, can get you through anything. And it surely did this summer.

* * *

I hate good-byes. I say this into my camera as I sit on my stoop.

I film Romy and Marisol as they climb into Aunt Sally's car. Mom gave them each a small duffel filled with stuff we collected on our shopping trips. Small things. Flats from 8th Street—which we got two for one. Candy from Li-Lac Chocolates. Souvenirs from the shop down in the Bowery. And of course, notebooks and matching pens from the Chinese mart. We did it all.

"Okay, Vi. Give us room," Dad says as he opens the front door. The Santrys are packed and ready to go. Dad helps Mr. Santry down the ramp in his wheelchair. When they get to the sidewalk, Dad leans over the chair as they have a private conversation. Dad nods his head a lot and smiles.

It is so cool that Dad and Mr. Santry have become friends. It's almost like my roomies and me—they just connected. Mom and Mrs. Santry were easygoing with each other too. All of us piled into this one old house—we had better all have gotten along, and we did! And more!

I help Suzanne with her duffel.

"This was the best trip ever." Suzanne gives me a hug. "Are you sure you don't want to come back to Prefect?"

"I'm gonna miss you guys. But who's going to stalk Tag Nachmanoff if I don't go back to LaGuardia?"

"Olivia Olson?"

"She doesn't have to stalk. She's *in*."

"Right." Suzanne watches as my dad helps Mr. Santry into the car. "Those two are like ketchup and fries."

"Yeah," I agree.

"You know, everything I observe in life is inspired by the Dairy Queen. How sad is that?" Suzanne laughs.

"Hey. You mastered the dip cone. Be grateful."

Suzanne climbs into the car next to her dad.

"Westward ho!" Mr. Santry calls out the window as Mrs. Santry backs out of our cul-de-sac. I watch for a moment in real time, and then remember my camera. I get the final shot of the station wagon as it pulls onto the boulevard. I can't say why exactly, but when it disappears into the traffic, I begin to cry.

FOURTEEN

GRAND DRIES WHILE I WASH THE DISHES. THROUGH the window, George, Mom, and Dad relax with coffee after dinner. It's Monday night, Grand and George's night off from the theater. Cleo is nosing around the fence line, thrilled to be in actual grass.

Mom and I spent the day putting the apartment downstairs back in spiffy order to rent it again. The Longfellows went back to England on the fumes of a great theatrical success.

Grand and George received excellent reviews, and the play is what they call "a summer sleeper." They can tell, after the first week, that it looks like *Arsenic and Old Lace* will have a long run. Evidently, there are plenty of people who love a good, standard straight play, and with Mr.

Longfellow's British touch, Daryl Roth hit it out of the park. The advance sales are healthy.

I can already see the changes that a hit play make in Grand's life. Financial security, at least in the short term, is good for an actress. She's upgrading her kitchen and painting the apartment. That's Grand. It's all about home. She has traveled so much all her life, she loves being in her apartment and settling in for a long run.

"Grand, how did you end up in New York City?"

"I was cast in *Antony and Cleopatra* at the Public Theater in 1966."

"I know. I meant, I guess, why did you stay?"

"Well, you know that my people were farmers in Ohio."

"Right."

"Well, I like cabbage as much as the next person, and that's where the similarities between me and my people begin and end. I always wanted more. I needed city life. So, I moved to Chicago in 1950"—she clears her throat and looks out into the yard at George—"in the sixties and went to work as a stenographer by day and an actress by night. I did some modeling for department stores, and then the acting caught on a bit, and I met your grandfather, and then we decided to try for the brass ring."

"And then you had Mom."

"Yes. My most beautiful surprise."

"You didn't plan on children?"

"Didn't think about it. But then, there she was. And she's been such a great daughter. And look! I got you out of the deal. That's the best part. I got you and I don't have to do a thing, just love you."

"Thank you for sending me to Prefect last year."

"Oh, please, you're welcome. And you've already thanked me in a million ways. I'm so proud of you. If you ever want to go back, you can. I have a nice steady job this year, and there's plenty to go around."

"Thanks. But I don't think I ever want to leave New York again. Not for long, anyhow." As I say this, I get a funny feeling in my stomach. Maybe I will spend time away from New York someday. I'll try and stay open to all possibilities.

"I understand. You can stay here for college. You'll study filmmaking; I surely hope you go to NYU. So we can be close always. And then you'll be off having your own life."

"I hope I have good luck."

"Oh, you don't need it. You're loved. That's all the luck you need."

"Hey," Andrew says from the hallway.

"We're in here," I holler back.

Andrew comes into the kitchen. "Hey, Grand, the blogosphere is full of cool stuff about your play."

"Really? What are the bloggers saying?"

"Long run. Great ensemble cast."

"Wonderful!"

"And there was this tasty tidbit about you and George."

Grand spins on her heel. "Really?"

"Says you and George are like Mae West and Cary Grant."

"What?" Grand is perplexed.

"You know, a team."

"Well, Mae West and Cary Grant weren't a team—Mae West claims she discovered Cary Grant."

"Maybe they mean that."

"But that is inaccurate," Grand says.

"I can write in."

"You do that. And you tell those blog people that the correct spin on my relationship with George is more a Lunt and Fontanne deal. Got it?"

"Can do."

Andrew pulls an envelope out of his back pocket. "Did you get your class sked?" he asks.

"I did."

"Are you going to do the editing class?"

"Are you?"

"Yeah."

"Then I'll do it too," I tell Andrew.

Grand stands. "Okay, kids, I'm going outside to put my feet up."

Cleo, who is now asleep under the kitchen table, rises up on her paws and shakes herself out. "Come on, Cleo," Grand says, holding the screen door open for her.

"Feel like going for a walk?" Andrew asks.

"Sure." I holler out the window, "I'm going for a walk with Andrew."

"Don't be late," Dad says in a fake menacing tone.

"I won't, Father Dearest."

I hear them laugh in the backyard. Andrew and I slip out the front and down the stoop.

"Want an ice cream?" Andrew asks.

"Dairy Delight."

"The fake stuff?"

"Yeah, it's good. They have real ice cream too."

"I'd rather have Baskin-Robbins," Andrew says.

"Okay, we'll go there and I'll have a diet soda."

"You aren't getting all girly on me with the dieting, are you?"

"No way. I had two chili dogs, french fries, and a cookie for dinner."

"I hate it when girls don't eat."

"I can't control all girls, Andrew."

"I know." He smiles. "I think we're going to get Mrs. Holloman for English this year."

"She's great."

"That's what I hear."

"How is Caitlin's schedule?"

"We only have her for lunch and stagecraft together. She has concert band and strings combo. You know she has to take that to get into Juilliard," Andrew explains.

"I know. By the way, she told me that she and Maurice write long letters to each other. On paper. With a pen and ink. Like my parents used to do."

"Still no email at the Pullapillys?"

"Maybe in a hundred years. I don't know what I'd do if I couldn't email the girls."

"You miss your roommates, don't you?"

"A lot."

"They were great."

"I thought you would fall in love with Suzanne."

"Why would you think that?"

"I don't know. Every boy does. And you know something? I'm happy for her. Watching her in the world is like looking at great architecture, or an amazing painting, or that feeling you get the first time you hear a perfect song. You're just happy to be in the presence of that particular thing. It's that way with Suzanne. It's just a gift to be around her."

"I feel that way about you."

"And I feel that way about you, too."

"Viola, sometimes I think you don't really understand."

"Understand what?"

"How I feel."

I am deeply insulted. "Are you kidding?"

"About most things, yeah, you get it, but some things you just ignore."

Okay, what is going on here? Andrew is being critical. He is almost never critical. So I ask, "Like what?"

"It's been all weird since I kissed you."

"Yeah?" The truth is, he's right. I am very confused about my feelings for Andrew. On the one hand, I see how perfectly good and kind he is, and how handsome. And I don't know how I'll feel when he gets a new girlfriend. I might hate it, or who knows, I might like her. For the most part, things have been completely fine, and just as they always have been, but that kiss really did seem like the end of one chapter and the start of a new one. The only problem is, I haven't really read the new chapter. I just sort of tossed the book off to the side, as though that key event were somehow The End.

"Do you ever wonder why?" he asks.

"Sure. It just took me by surprise, I guess. I think you missed me when I was at school, and you were leaving for camp, but you got overwhelmed."

"That's not true."

"Well, that's what *I* think is true."

"Okay, fair enough," Andrew says.

"Are we arguing about this?"

"No, no, not at all," Andrew says, lowering his voice as if to prove the point that this is not an argument. "Wouldn't it be great if we started LaGuardia this year in a whole new way?"

"In what way?"

"I don't know. Like going together."

"Like dating?"

"Yeah."

Andrew wants me to be his GF. I think back over the summer, and when I wasn't running interference for Caitlin and Maurice, is it possible that Andrew was trying to get my attention? Well, he did kiss me, and then he went on to have a GF at summer camp, which I took as a sign that he wasn't interested in me in that way. When he came home, he broke up with Mel, and came over every day, and even dropped everything to tour the city with my roomies. I don't have a single other guy friend who would do that. Only Andrew.

"Well, what do you think?" Andrew says as he opens the door to the ice-cream shop for me.

"I think we're BFFAAs, and I don't want to ruin that." I feel a huge sense of relief being honest and saying that out loud.

"I worry about that too."

"Then, I guess, if you have to have an answer, I would say that I'm not ready."

"Okay," Andrew says. "Now I feel pretty dopey that I brought it up at all."

"It's not dopey. I think it's refreshing to know that there's a guy in the world who actually knows what he is feeling and speaks up."

Andrew smiles. "Only with you."

"That makes me feel very special."

"Because you are," he says.

This is the moment in all ice-cream runs when something is said that triggers the next moment, which leads to A Kiss. But Andrew doesn't move toward me, nor do I toward him. The bright lights in this corner shop, along with the scent of vanilla, do not inspire kissing, but the opposite, loud chatter and histrionics. Plus, I've asked for more time, and Andrew is absolutely willing to give it to me.

* * *

School starts in a couple of weeks, and almost on cue, autumn arrives. Overnight, it seems, I don't need the fan in my room. The night breeze pushes the blade around, making a soft clicking sound. I probably won't turn it on again, and I'll remember to take it out in the morning and put it back in the closet, until next summer.

I go online to check my emails. One from Romy. Three from Marisol, including a forward about keeping a pink woman running across the screen to raise money for the cure for breast cancer; two from LaGuardia High School with announcements about class schedules; and then a new one, from Kevin Santry. I never get emails from Suzanne's brothers, so I open it first.

Dear Viola,

My mom asked me to email you and your parents. We are at Chicago General Hospital with Dad. He has taken a bad turn and is very sick. The doctors are not hopeful. Mom wanted you to know. We are all here with him. When he was still talking, he told us all about the trip to New York. He had the time of his life.

Anyhow, we will keep you posted. Suzanne is not checking her phone. She is, as you can imagine, beyond upset. In fact, this is hitting her the hardest. If you can let her friends know, we would appreciate it. We will be in touch. Love, Kevin

I reread the email. I freeze, not knowing what to do. So first, I paste it and send it to Marisol and Romy. Then, without closing the computer, I run into my parents' bedroom. Mom is reading and Dad is watching TV. I look at them, so normal in their bed, perfectly healthy, and I burst into tears.

Mom jumps out of the bed and comes to me, putting her arms around me.

"What happened?" she asks.

"Mr. Santry."

FIFTEEN

THE DRIVE TO CHICAGO, WHICH WOULD UNDER ANY other circumstances be fun, is a blur. The fields of Pennsylvania give way to Ohio, and as we go through Indiana, I remember the day my parents dropped me off at the Prefect Academy. We are in Chicago by nightfall.

There is something soothing about being in the car with my parents. When the call came that Mr. Santry had died, it was Mrs. Santry who called. She wanted Mom and Dad to know how much their new friendship meant to Mr. Santry. That's just like her—like the whole Santry family really. They are thinking about everyone else's feelings, while they are in the worst of their grief.

Suzanne and I talked on the phone, but I did most of the talking. She was very quiet and cried a lot. I just let her cry. When we hung up, I had a good cry too.

Mom, Dad, and I are staying at a hotel in Oak Park, near the Santrys' home. Mrs. Santry asked us to stay with them, but Mom wouldn't hear of it.

The room is nice, blue wall-to-wall carpeting, a blue flowered bedspread, and beige curtains. I crawl into one of the two beds while Dad and Mom tend to their funeral outfits. Dad is hanging his suit; Mom irons a blouse.

I am wearing a dress that, strangely enough, Suzanne gave to me. It's a beautiful hand-me-down, a simple black dress with a plain black belt.

I email Romy and Marisol, whose parents decided that they couldn't afford the same trip twice in two weeks, because the girls are due back at Prefect for the fall semester. I'm going to represent them at the funeral, as they would do for me in the same situation.

"Mom, do you think I should give them the DVD of the footage I cut?" I spent the last couple of days with Andrew, making a story out of the New York trip with the Santrys, Romy, and Marisol. We added some music, some of Mr. Santry's favorites, including "Waltzing Matilda," which he used to play a lot.

"Absolutely," Mom says.

Once we're unpacked at the hotel, we get back into the car to go over to the Santrys' house. Mrs. Santry is having dinner brought in, and the neighbors (evidently) have dropped off enough cakes and pies to last the year.

Strangely, I know my way to the house. I actually know the turn off the circle, and can pick the street. Dad makes the turn, and it's easy to find the house. It's the one with all the cars parked outside.

Dad finds a spot and we get out of our car. Mom and Dad make their way to the walkway. I can't move. Mom turns to me. "Honey?"

I still can't move.

Mom and Dad come back to me, by the car.

"What's wrong, honey?" Dad says.

"I never knew anyone who died." I begin to cry.

Mom and Dad put their arms around me. "We're so sorry."

"This is part of life. And we wish you never had to face it," Mom says.

"You're only fifteen," Dad says. "And we were hoping that you'd be older when you had to deal with this."

"I feel horrible for Suzanne," I tell them. "Because I can't imagine the world without you."

Mom and Dad hold on to me for a long time. Their embrace gives me the courage to walk up the sidewalk into the house. We push the door open. The Santry home, just as it was last Thanksgiving, is filled with laughter, and music, and lights. I look at Mom and Dad.

"This wake is like the man himself," Dad says. "Full of joy."

I can see Suzanne through the doorway to the kitchen. Mrs. Santry is putting out food. Kevin and Joe are busy attending to guests. She sees me, excuses herself from talking with a small group, and runs to me.

"Suz, I'm so sorry," I tell her as we embrace.

"Thank you for coming. My dad thought the world of you," she says in my ear. Then Suzanne hugs my parents. "Dad felt he found long-lost friends when he met you. Thank you for New York."

Suzanne takes us into the kitchen and introduces us to cousins, aunts and uncles, and friends from the neighborhood.

"You must be so tired," Mrs. Santry says to us.

"No, we're doing just fine. How are you?" Dad asks her.

"It's hard."

"Bob was a great guy," Dad says.

"Oh, he felt he found a brother in you, Adam," Mrs. Santry assures him.

"Is there anything we can do?" Dad asks.

"You have done too much already. You came all this way. I can't tell you what it means to our family."

I reach into my purse. "Mrs. Santry, this is the DVD of the movies we made when you came to New York." I place it in her hands. She looks down at it, as a person would who has waited a long time for a letter, some correspondence that was lost, and suddenly found. She holds the DVD close to her heart. "Thank you." She gives me a hug. "And thank you," she says to my parents, tears brimming in her eyes.

After the wake, we walk back to our car, and the first chill of fall settles on us.

"Dad?"

"Yeah, hon?"

"That wasn't bad at all."

"No, it wasn't, was it?" Mom says.

"What were you expecting?" Dad asks.

"I was afraid they would be so sad that they wouldn't know what to say to us. And I would never know what to say to them."

"Viola, sometimes, and you just learned this—all you can do is show up. Just be present when you're needed, and that means more than anything you could ever say."

Me: Are you up?

AB: Waiting to hear from you.

Me: Funeral this morning.

AB: *How is Suzanne?*

Me: A wreck but strong.

AB: *How are you?*

Me: A wreck but strong.

AB: *You'll be okay. Hang tough.*

Me: Thanks. I gave Mrs. Santry our DVD.

AB: *I never heard "Waltzing Matilda" before.*

Me: Dad loves it. He loves folk music.

AB: *It was easy to find on iTunes.*

Me: Mom is calling me to get ready. So, gotta go.

AB: *Hey, Vi?*

Me: Yeah.

AB: *Being BFFAAs is totally enough for me.*

Me: Thanks.

AB: *Nothing has changed.*

You think life is one thing, that it's going one way, but that just isn't the case. I swore that Tag Nachmanoff would stay cute, that I'd always be good at math. I swore I'd never leave Brooklyn, and I did, to go to Prefect. And I was certain that my yellow flats would never go out of style. I took too much for granted. I didn't believe that change applied to me as long as I stayed put. But Mr. Santry's death shows you never know. You just never know.

* * *

Andrew, who is usually right about everything, is wrong about change. Everything is changing. We are trying to hold on to a lot of things, and none of them are stable. Suzanne is going to finish high school and then college without her dad. It seems so unfair.

I'm surprised when Caitlin logs on to IM right when Andrew and I are saying good-bye.

CP: Give my love to Suzanne.

Me: I will.

CP: Maurice sends his best.

Me: Is Mom letting you e?

CP: Yes, from time to time.

Me: Good!

CP: If Maurice lived in Brooklyn, no way!

Me: I know.

CP: Mom and Dad are better now. They want you and Andrew to hang here where they can keep an eye on us.

Me: Fabulous.

CP: I'm laughing.

Me: I'm sure you are.

Mr. Santry's funeral is my first ever. My parents only go to church on Christmas and for funerals. Technically, we are Episcopalians, but it's more generic than that. We go to whatever church has the best music at holidays.

The Santrys are Methodists. The church is very plain, yet pretty. Stained-glass windows, walnut benches, and simple chairs around a plain table altar. We join the throng going into the church. Mr. Santry has a standing-room-only funeral.

I feel oddly comforted by wearing Suzanne's hand-me-down. There is no casket at the service, as Mr. Santry was cremated. There's just a large framed photograph of him with his family on the altar. It's a blowup of the one that Suzanne kept on her nightstand at Prefect. It's black and white. Everyone is beautiful. Everyone is laughing. And Mr. Santry is sitting in a regular chair and doesn't look one bit sick.

The family files in, and it's as though there is no time for tears. They stop and talk to people in the aisles as they make their way to the front.

Then the minister says a prayer. Mom and Dad bow their heads, and so do I. Then Kevin makes his way to the lectern.

"My dad taught me the important things in life. How to bait a hook. How to throw a baseball. And how to ask a girl to the prom. But I would say the biggest lesson he taught me was how to live. He threw himself into everything he did. He never let illness or sadness or defeat define his life, or who he was. Rather, his idea of success was just to keep going, keep moving forward. . . .

"This summer he and my mom and my sister went to New York City. He had a rough month before they left, but somehow, the trip, and the anticipation of seeing the city with his good friends, gave him the energy he needed to see it through. Suzanne's friend Viola shot some film when they were there, and last night she left this with my mother. We all watched it, and to see our dad in the city, even rowing a canoe in Central Park, reminded us of how strong and determined he was, but also, that he knew how to have fun. So, we'd like to show it to you now."

The minister and Kevin pull a screen forward. Mom takes my hand on one side, and my dad's on the other. They lower the lights, and the opening guitar riff of "Waltzing Matilda" scores the opening shot of the Santrys' arrival in New York. There are wolf whistles and cheers as the scenes unfold. Central Park Lake, romantic kisses between Mr. and Mrs. Santry, at night in our yard, when the parents had wine, and then during the day as we covered New York City like New Year's confetti.

As the final shot goes into close-up, the frame freezes

(Andrew's idea) on Mr. Santry laughing. The mourners exhale one breath together as they look up at him. The image of him laughing, enjoying his life, and enjoying those he loved on an adventure to New York City says everything about the man. A movie can do that. An image can say it all.

Sometimes I think my camera is my friend. Sometimes I think it's my diary. And sometimes, like today, I realize it has a higher purpose—to record what people feel.

No matter how sad I am for Suzanne and her family, I can't help but be happy that I got to know Mr. Santry. And no, it wasn't for long, but it sure was important, and I will never forget him.

The entire population of Chicago is crammed into the Santry home. Or at least it seems that way. Suzanne has been cornered by her great-aunt and cousins. Mom and Dad want to get on the road in daylight, so I rescue her from her relatives.

Suzanne hugs me. "Thank you for coming."

"I'll always be here for you," I promise.

"And I will always be here for you," Suzanne promises right back.

I wish I didn't have to leave her. I wish that all my

friends lived in one city, and that we could run a few blocks to visit anytime we wished. But part of growing up is expanding your world (as my dad likes to say), and my world has definitely grown.

"I'll miss you at Prefect," Suzanne says.

"You're going back?"

"It's what my dad wanted. And I love it there." She smiles.

"I understand." And I do. Once I got to know my roommates, I loved Prefect. And I'll never forget it.

I run down the walkway from the Santrys' porch to the street. Their street looks like a used car lot, double-parked all the way down, with people visiting after the funeral. Dad taps on the horn. I climb into our car. I look back at the Santry house, full of people, full of love.

Dad and I have a running joke about Mom. All she has to do is sit in a car, and she instantly falls asleep. I lean forward between Dad, who is driving, and Mom, who occasionally snores.

We are going through the blackest portion of Pennsylvania—aka farm country—on our way back home to Brooklyn.

"You did a wonderful thing, Vi. Your movie made the funeral."

"Not really. I just make movies of everything."

"That was really special."

"He was a good man, Dad."

"I know," Dad says. A truck blows past us, filling the car with bright light, and speeds down the highway.

"I was thinking, Dad."

"What?"

"Would it hurt your feelings if I went back to boarding school?"

"Where did that come from?"

"I don't know."

"Are you serious?"

"Yeah." I take a deep breath. "I've been thinking about it since Grand said she would send me anywhere I wanted to go. She's making good money now."

"Thank goodness for rent control," Dad says wryly.

"Grand believes in education. Says it's the best place to put your money."

Dad adjusts the rearview mirror so he can see my face. "She's right. But you have a place at LaGuardia."

"I know."

"You know, you shouldn't go back because you feel bad for Suzanne. You should go back because it's the right place for you at the right time in your life."

"It'll kill Mom, won't it?"

"The way things are going, she'll sleep through it."

"You're hilarious, Dad."

"Marry a funny guy, Viola. We age well."

"Okay, Dad."

"We'll have to check if Prefect still has a spot for you."

"I know."

"You won't be disappointed if they can't take you?"

"They'll take me."

"How do you know?"

"Dad, I'm getting intuitive."

"Really?"

"Yeah. Grand says you have to look at the patterns in your life."

"Fifteen years isn't really long enough for a pattern to develop."

"It already has. Things happen to me out of the blue."

"That's interesting."

"You took a job with Mom in Afghanistan, and that led me to Prefect. And then I met my roommates, and now I can't imagine my life without them. See? Fate. And it's a pattern. I don't ask for change, it just comes to me."

"I get it."

"I knew you would."

"So, I'm going to lose you to Indiana?"

"I'll be home on holidays."

"Right." Dad smiles. "What are you going to tell Andrew?"

"Andrew's my BFFAAPK."

"PK?"

"Post-kiss," I explain. "But don't worry. It was just one kiss, over and out."

"Okay." Dad adjusts his glasses. "I get it."

"Are you sure that you do, Dad?"

"Oh yeah. Team Adam is on your side."

I throw my arms around Dad and kiss him on the cheek. Mom stirs and wakes up. She sits up in her seat. "What'd I miss?"

"Viola made a big decision," Dad says.

Mr. Pullapilly opens the door to the apartment. "Come on in, Viola," he says. "Caitlin!"

Caitlin comes out of her bedroom and waves for me to join her. I enter her room, neat as a pin, with a simple twin bed and a giant mirror over it. I sit down on the edge of it.

"Have you heard from Maurice?" I ask.

Caitlin smiles and goes to a small box, embroidered with metallic stars. She opens it. There, nestled in the satin, is a stack of letters from Maurice.

"Wow."

"He writes beautiful letters about school and his friends. Mr. Longfellow just got a new job. He's directing a revival of a Harold Pinter play."

"Good for him!"

"It's all perfect. If only Maurice lived here." Caitlin's dark brown eyes fill with sadness. "Oh well. Someday. Right?"

"Absolutely," I assure her. "I don't want to make things worse, but I've made a decision. I have something to tell you."

Caitlin closes the letter box and looks at me.

"I'm going back to Prefect."

"Suzanne needs you?"

"Yes, but that's not why I'm going. I'm going back because I like it. And I belong there. I think I have more to learn about myself."

"I wish you would stay and learn about yourself here."

I laugh, and then Caitlin laughs too.

"I will always be your friend, Viola. Wherever you go. Wherever I go. I hope you know that."

"I count on it." I give Caitlin a hug.

"Have you told Andrew?"

I shake my head that I haven't. "I hope he understands."

"It won't be easy. But he always wants what is best for you."

* * *

Andrew sits in the backyard under the grape arbor, checking his BlackBerry. It took Mom and me longer to get back from Target than we expected. Back-to-school at Target is, like, a zoo. And I needed a lot of stuff to go back to Prefect.

Mrs. Zidar pulled, like, a million strings to put our quad back together intact. We played the grief card, which maybe we shouldn't have, but I made the point that Suzanne is going to be going through enough change, could we please keep our living situation consistent?

"Here." I toss Andrew a bag of cotton candy from Target.

"My favorite," he says.

"I know."

"Are you going back to boarding school so you don't have to go out with me?"

"Who told you?"

"Your dad. He figured you told me already."

"I meant to."

"Well, is it true? You're running away? Sort of? Kind of?"

"Andrew."

"That's a no." He looks off.

"That's a big no. I can't even tell you what you mean

to me. You mean more to me than any boyfriend ever would."

"Seriously?" Andrew looks at me. He shoves his BlackBerry into his pocket and turns to face me.

"Totally seriously. You know, Andrew, you can be awfully rigid."

"I am not."

"You get an idea in your head and that's it. It's like Cleo with a tube sock. You just grip with your teeth and you don't let go."

"I know what I want." He rips into the bag of cotton candy.

"And I don't."

"You know you want to go to Prefect."

"That I know for sure. But it's the rest of it I'm not so sure about."

"It's okay."

"Really?"

"Yeah, the cotton candy is just okay. It's better on Coney Island when it's fresh."

"Sorry."

"I'm kidding."

"I know," I tell him. And I do know. I know Andrew Bozelli. Inside and out.

* * *

Dad is not happy to have to get back in the car with Mom and me and drive out to the Midwest. But the truth is, he'd drive anywhere to make me happy, or Mom happy. He's just that kind of a guy.

My duffels are stacked by the doorway of my room. The box with my computer stuff is neatly placed. My clothes for the drive back are laid out on my chair.

I turn off my laptop. As I go to shut it off, the wallpaper is a picture of Romy, Suzanne, Marisol, and me at the fountain in Central Park. We are sitting there in a row, like a quartet of dorks. It's summer in the park, it's hot out, and we're all sweaty. Our hair is stringy and gross, but we're smiling. Soon, we'll all be back together again.

Even Mrs. Pullapilly had to admit that every chance meeting leads a person to make a decision that becomes part of a grand plan, a plan that creates the forward motion of your life.

New York will always be here, the trains, the rooftops, the skyline, and the people, and any road I take will get me where I'm going, and then, when I've learned all I need to know, those same roads will lead me home.

The cloudless periwinkle sky of Indiana has become as nurturing to me as the waves of the East River, and the fields of green, square and perfect, like patches on a handmade quilt, have become as majestic to me as the skyline of Manhattan lit from within like a constellation of silver stars.

Mr. Santry died, and that makes me want to *never ever* leave my parents, but that is not good for them, or for me.

I have to learn to walk in this world alone, but my destination must always be into the arms of those who really love me. Friendship has opened up my life. It's taught me how to be in the world. It's shown me what I like and don't, what I will stand up for and what I won't. I can't imagine my life without my friends.

It's a brave thing to go back to school in Indiana, because it scares me. A higher goal is always reached by overcoming fear.

Only *you* know for sure what is right for you. Grand calls it "honoring your inner voice," my mom calls it "keeping your own counsel," and Caitlin's aunt Naira calls it the "wise whispering wind." Well, whatever it is, and however it can be defined in Brooklyn, South Bend, or India, *something* is calling me to go back to Prefect and finish what I started.

And while my heart breaks to leave those I love and return to Indiana, New York City will always be here.

I know that Grand has George and Cleo and a long run

in a good play, Andrew has Caitlin, and Mom and Dad have each other and their work, and no matter where I go, I have all of them forever. There's email, telephone, and breaks.

I am so lucky. I have the family I was born into, and the family I chose.

Romy, Suzanne, and Marisol would've been just fine without me, but now we don't have to find out. We'll be together again.

This school year, there are going to be some changes. I'm taking the top bunk. I want to be closer to the sky. Closer to the pink moon. And closer to the stars that shine over South Bend, which turn out to be the very same ones that twinkle over Brooklyn.

ACKNOWLEDGMENTS

I dedicate this book to my holy trinity of librarians who were instrumental in guiding my reading choices as a girl. James Varner, the Wise County Bookmobile Librarian, introduced me to Pippi Longstocking by Astrid Lindgren, as well as other books about high-spirited girls on a mission to live on their own terms.

Ernestine Roller encouraged me to read all of the American patriots series by various authors under the Bobbs-Merrill banner, as well as everything written by the great Beverly Cleary and brilliant Madeleine L'Engle. Mrs. Roller also recommended *Harriet the Spy* by Louise Fitzhugh, which shaped my desire to become a writer and to someday live in New York City. Mrs. Roller was more than my Big Stone Gap Elementary School librarian, she was also a dream maker.

Perhaps the greatest influence on me as a teenage reader was Ms. Billie Jean Scott, the Powell Valley High School librarian who encouraged me to push the boundaries of my reading. When I read *Jane Eyre,* she gave me *Wide Sargasso Sea* to show me how stories can be told from various points of view by the same characters in the hands of different authors. Ms. Scott hooked me on the Transcendentalist movement. To this day, I turn to Henry David Thoreau, Ralph Waldo Emerson, and the Alcott sisters for inspiration.

Ms. Scott kept a portable blackboard in the library. Each week she would (in perfect Palmer penmanship!) select one thought from a great book and write it on that board. Day after day during study period, I would look up at the sentence she chose and think about why she selected it—and how one sentence is the building block of a good book. Ms. Scott's influence upon my work is incalculable.

I owe all three librarians a great debt as they were artful professionals, who made the library (including one on wheels) sacred spaces to be shared by a community hungry to learn. They could not have been happier when Big Stone Gap opened The Slemp Memorial Library in the 1970s. They knew that a town with a library was not only lucky, but committed to the greater good. Our public libraries are our national treasures.

My evermore thanks to the great team at HarperTeen. I am lucky to work with a fabulous editor, Tara Weikum. Thank you also to the sensational Susan Katz, Kate Jackson, Elise Howard, Melissa Miller, Barb Fitzsimmons, Alison Donalty, Ray Shappell, Diane Naughton, Christina Colangelo, Kristina Radke, Colleen O'Connell, Sandee Roston, Cindy Hamilton, Laura Lutz, Andrea Pappenheimer, Kerry Moynagh, Kathy Faber, Liz Frew, Jessica Abel, Josh Weiss, Gwen Morton, and Melinda Weigel.

My thanks and admiration to my UK team: the great Ian Chapman, my fabulous editor Suzanne Baboneau, and the irreplaceable Nigel Stoneman.

Love and unending gratitude to my William Morris Endeavor Team: Suzanne Gluck, Caroline Donofrio, Mina Shaghaghi, Eugenie Furniss, Claudia Webb, Tracy Fisher, Laura Bonner, Covey Crolius, Alicia Gordon, Stephanie Ward, Cara Stein, Amanda Krentzman, and Nancy Josephson.

I am grateful to Jean Morrissey for her eagle eyes.

Larry Sanitsky is my favorite producer, thank you also to Claude Chung at the Sanitsky Company.

Thank you to the world's best assistant, Kelly Meehan. Thank you also to: the world's best intern, Allison Von Groesbeck, our summer intern, Emma Morrissey, and our swing helper, Molly McGuire.

When it comes to all things theatrical, thank you to the great talents that encouraged me: director Ed Stern, Charles Randolph Wright, Daryl Roth, George Keathley, Theo Barnes, Jerry Fargo, Donna De Matteo, Rosemary DeAngelis, and in loving memory of Vincent Gugleotti and Ruth Goetz.

When we were photographing the cover of this book on a sunny day in Greenwich Village, Cay Blau was walking her King Charles Spaniel, Cleo, in Greenwich Village. Cleo was so adorable she posed for the cover and became a character in this novel. It just goes to show you—life is full of surprises, and sometimes all you have to do is show up.

Also by Adriana Trigiani

Young Adult Fiction

Viola in Reel Life

Fiction

Brava, Valentine

Very Valentine

Home to Big Stone Gap

Rococo

The Queen of the Big Time

Lucia, Lucia

Milk Glass Moon

Big Cherry Holler

Big Stone Gap

Nonfiction

Don't Sing at the Table: Life Lesson from My Grandmothers

Cooking with My Sisters (co-author)